A Tragic Pa

A Psychic Café

(Book 6)

By

April Fernsby

www.aprilfernsby.com

1. http://www.coverkicks.com

Chapter 1

"Are you sure about this?" I asked my younger sister, Erin. "You could be doing something more relaxing on a Sunday afternoon." My gaze went to her stomach.

Erin clicked her fingers. "Hey, my eyes are up here. Stop looking at my tummy."

I smiled. "I can't help it. It's so beautiful and round. Why do you look so radiant? When I was eight months pregnant, I looked exhausted. It's not fair. You're having twins. You should have the decency to look a little bit tired."

Her eyes sparkled. "I feel amazing. Like I could take on the world. The twins must be giving me superpowers. I'm ready for anything."

I looked around the deserted café which we co-owned. Erin had decorated it from floor to ceiling with colourful streamers, balloons, and banners in preparation for a birthday party. There were images of rainbow-coloured unicorns everywhere. Which was perfect for the unicorn-loving girl who was having her party here.

"How well do you know Primrose Olson?" I asked.

"Who?" Erin moved over to a banner and straightened it.

"The birthday girl. The one who's going to be six," I prompted. "The one who loves unicorns."

"Oh, I don't know her at all. I assume she's like all six-year-old girls. Have we got enough banners? I've got some more in the kitchen. What about balloons? Are there enough?"

I said, "You don't need any more decorations. It already looks like a rainbow exploded in here. And that rainbow brought a hundred other rainbows with it."

"Don't exaggerate, Karis. Have we got enough food? I can always make more. Did I tell you I've made separate food for the children and adults? And tell me the truth about the unicorn cake. Does it look fabulous?"

"It's the most amazing unicorn cake I've ever seen," I answered truthfully. "Erin, does the birthday girl actually like unicorns? Or are you just assuming that?"

"She loves unicorns. According to her mum anyway." Erin absentmindedly ran her hand lovingly over her extended stomach. "I think we could use more balloons. I'll go into the kitchen and get some."

I walked over to her and placed my hands on her shoulders. I gently guided her to a chair and sat her down. "Stop fussing. Stop doing things. You should be resting more."

She stood back up. "I can't rest. I've got so much to do! This is the first time we've had a children's party here. I want everything to go well."

"And it will. How did Primrose's mum get in touch with you? Was it via our website?"

Erin gave me a look of despair. "I met her at an antenatal class. Robbie made me go. I told him I didn't need to, but he insisted and said it would be good for me to get to know other parents."

"He's right. I'm still in touch with friends I made at my antenatal classes."

She grinned. "It wasn't me who made lots of new friends. It was Robbie. He came with me. He was in his element talking to the other mums and dads about everything baby-related. And it was him who started a conversation with Klaudia and Dean Olson. Klaudia's pregnant with her second, and she said she was too tired to organise a party for her Primrose. So, Robbie offered to hold it here."

Knowing how kind-hearted my brother-in-law is, I immediately asked, "I hope we're charging for this party."

"We certainly are. Unicorn decorations don't come cheap." Her nose wrinkled. "I wasn't keen on the idea at first. I didn't want a load of excited children running around the café. Not when we've spent so much time and money renovating this building."

"But it'll be a good experience for us. And if it goes well, we could get some more bookings."

"That's exactly what Robbie said." She looked left and right even though there was no one around, and said quietly, "They smell. Don't you think they smell?"

"Who?"

"Children. Especially the little ones. Robbie and I went to a primary school last week for a look around. I told him it was too soon to put the twins down for a school, but he said it's never too early to be organised. Do you know, I caught him looking at universities the other day. Anyway, when we went to that primary school, I almost threw up! The stink that came from the classrooms was overpowering."

"It could be your hormones making your sense of smell more sensitive."

"I hope so." Her face filled with disgust. "One of them touched me. A little boy. He grabbed my hand. He was all sticky. I hope the ones coming here today won't be sticky. Or smelly. Or noisy. I don't want any of those in our lovely, clean café."

I shook my head. "They're all like that. At least, to some extent. You'll have to get used to it."

"But what if I don't?" Her voice held a hint of fear. "What if I can't cope with children at all? Even my own? What if I'm a terrible mother who can't stand the smell of them? I'll be like one of those witches from that Roald Dahl story, the ones who hate children." She sat back down.

Her eyes filled with tears. "I'm going to be a witch of a mother. I just know it."

I wrapped my arms around her. "You're going to be marvellous. Your husband is a big child, and look how much you love him. And how you look after him."

She blinked her tears away, and gave me a wobbly smile. "He's easy to love." She rested both hands on her stomach. "If these two are as wonderful as my husband, then how can I fail to love them?"

"Is someone talking about me?" a friendly voice called over. "I thought I felt my ears burning. I hope you were saying kind things about me."

"Of course we were." Erin smiled over at her husband. "Have you sorted it out?"

Robbie ambled over to us, his customary smile on his face. "I have. There is now a safety gate in place. No one under the age of twelve should be able to get it open. I had a bit of trouble opening it myself."

I frowned. "A safety gate? Where?"

"At the bottom of the steps that lead to the first floor," Robbie explained. "We don't want any little people up there. There are too many dangerous areas. We've made everything child-safe down here, but it was easier to put a gate up rather than sorting everything out upstairs. The safety of little people is one of my priorities today." He sat opposite Erin and took her hands in his. His eyes were full of love. "Taking care of you is my top priority. How are you feeling, my delicate flower?"

I didn't hear Erin's reply, because my attention was drawn to the steps which now had a safety gate at the bottom of them. Something wasn't right. I could sense it. A sudden chill ran down my back, and my vision began to blur.

I knew what was happening. I was getting a psychic vision. And it wasn't going to be a pleasant one.

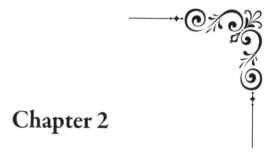

Chapter 2

I slowly walked towards the steps, my sense of unease growing. I saw the safety gate which Robbie had put there. It looked sturdy, but as I stared at it, it slowly opened. Of it's own accord.

A noise from the top of the steps made me jump. It almost sounded like a chuckle. But there was no one there.

Then I saw a shadow appear on the top step; a shadow which wasn't attached to anyone. The shadow loomed over the top step, and it was impossible to see if the blurred figure was male or female. A distorted shape at the top part of the shadow made me think there was a hat there.

Another chuckle sounded out as the apparition walked down the stairs. When it reached the third step, the shadow suddenly jerked, almost as if someone had pushed it.

The shadow's arms shot out, and it began to fall forwards. An almost imperceptible scream sounded out. It was no more than a whisper of a sound.

I watched in horror as the shadow tumbled helplessly down the steps and landed at my feet. Part of the shadow covered my shoes making me shiver.

The shape was still indistinct even though it was so close to me now. And it didn't move. I had the strongest feeling it was dead, even though that was a silly thing to say about a shadow.

Slowly, the shadow melted away. The safety gate closed, again on its own.

I nearly jumped out of my skin when someone touched my elbow. It was Erin.

She said, "Karis, what is it? Have you just had a vision?"

I gave her a slow nod. "I saw a shadow fall down the steps. And when it got to the bottom, it didn't move."

Erin paled. "Was it male or female?"

"I don't know." I swallowed. "I think I witnessed a death."

"A past death? Or one which is going to happen soon?'

I shrugged. "I don't know."

"Do you think it's a...you know...a murder?"

Once more, I shrugged. "Considering all the other murder visions I've had, you'd think I'd know what a murder looks like by now, wouldn't you?" I opened the safety gate. "Something happened to the shadow on the third step down. Let me check the step."

"I'll come with you."

I put my hand out. "You certainly will not. Stay right there."

Robbie came over and saw our concerned expressions. "What's going on? I only nipped into the kitchen for a coffee, and I come out to find you two looking scared witless."

Erin pointed at me, and said, "She's had a murder vision."

Robbie let out a heavy sigh. "Oh, Karis. Did you have to?"

"I'm sorry, but you know I can't control them."

Erin continued, "And she saw something happen to the shadow on the third step down. She's going up there to have a closer look, and she won't let me go with her."

Robbie said, "Of course she won't. And quite right too." He put his cup down on a nearby table. "Karis, I'll have a look at the suspicious third step. There could be an uneven bit of wood or a nail sticking up. I don't want you getting hurt. You stay here with your sister."

"No. I need to have a look for myself." I headed up the steps before he could argue. I heard Robbie following me.

I neared the top, and stopped at the fourth step down, knelt on it, and carefully placed my hand on the step above it. I braced myself, expecting a shock of some sort. But nothing happened. All I could feel was the smoothness of the wood beneath my fingertips.

Robbie crouched at my side. His eyebrows rose in question. "Well?"

I shook my head. "Nothing. It feels normal. I could have sworn this was where the shadow started to fall. It jerked forward like it was pushed."

"And what were you expecting to feel?"

I looked again at the step. "I don't know. Just something. Leftover energy perhaps."

"Isn't that good then?"

"I don't know." I looked back at Robbie. "What should we do? We can't have a murder here. Certainly not in the middle of a children's party."

Robbie said, "But that's not how it works, is it? Don't your visions always come true?"

I nodded. "But sometimes they're visions from the past, and I don't always know why I'm receiving them until later."

He gave me a reassuring smile. "Let's hope that's the case here."

I returned his smile even though I had a feeling that something terrible was going to happen soon, and there was nothing I could do to stop it.

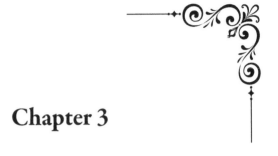

Chapter 3

I didn't have time to worry about a possible imminent death because the party guests began to arrive. One minute, the café was an oasis of calm, and the next it was full of chattering children and flustered parents.

Robbie was full of charm as he welcomed the birthday party in. He took control of everything, and soon had the children sitting in a semicircle near the window while he read them a story. Erin and I helped the parents with their coats and many bags. It seemed the smaller the child, the bigger the bag. We quickly served hot and cold drinks to the parents. We didn't interrupt the children because they were hanging on to Robbie's every word as he regaled them with an intriguing tale about a princess going into space and meeting aliens.

From the back of the room, Erin muttered to me, "Look at them. Those little people. They already look sticky and grubby. And I can smell them from here. Can you?"

I smiled at her. "They smell just like children do. You'll get used to it."

Her nose wrinkled. "I won't. Do they sell air freshener for children? I'll have to buy some."

The door opened, and an unlikely couple entered. An elderly woman in a tartan coat, and a handsome man with twinkly eyes. By the look of it, the woman was giving the man an ear-bashing about something or other. He looked my way, and discreetly rolled his eyes.

The unlikely couple came over to us.

The elderly woman was Peggy Marshall. A very dear friend and neighbour. I'd known her all my life, and she was like a second mum to Erin and me. The man was Seb. His official title was DCI Sebastian Parker. We had a complicated history. We had dated in our youth. Then fallen out big time in our teenage years. But we'd recently met up again, put the past behind us, and started dating again. It was still early days for us, but my feelings for him were growing stronger each day.

As Peggy took her tartan coat off, she nodded in Seb's direction, and said, "Would you believe this fella here? I told him not to take that road by the hospital. I told him it was visiting time and the roads would be chock-a-block, but would he listen? No, he wouldn't. And now we're the last ones here."

Seb shrugged. "I am only human. I make mistakes."

Peggy tutted at him. "You needn't have made any mistakes if you'd have listened to me in the first place."

"I'll try to do better in the future," Seb said earnestly. He placed a hand over his heart to add conviction to his words.

Peggy broke into a chuckle. "You'd better." She cast a soft look at Erin. "How are you? Still looking radiant. Not like Karis here when she was pregnant. She looked like the walking dead."

I shook my head at Peggy. "It's a good job I love you so much."

Erin rested her hand on her stomach. "I feel great." She lowered her voice. "But I can't stand the smell of children. Is that normal? Is it a pregnancy thing?"

"Could be." Peggy cast a glance at the sitting children. "Your Robbie has captivated them. He's going to make a smashing dad."

Erin let out a heavy sigh. "I know, but I'm not sure I'm going to make a good mum."

Peggy cupped Erin's cheek, and said with a tenderness which almost made me cry, "You are going to make an excellent mother. A wonderful mother. You have a heart overflowing with love, and that love has been waiting for your babies for years."

Erin's eyes glistened with tears. "Thanks, Peggy."

"Any time, my special girl." Peggy looked at Seb. "Well, are you going to get me a cup of tea, then? I need it after driving five hours to get here."

Seb replied, "It took us twenty-two minutes, Mrs Marshall. And every minute flew by in your delightful company."

"I know it did. Milk, no sugar. Thank you."

The door opened again making us look that way. A vision of beauty stood there in the form of a tall woman. She looked about my age, possibly younger. Her short auburn hair was cut in a bob which perfectly framed her heart-shaped face. Her make-up was expertly applied, and she had that healthy dewy look which I'd never been able to achieve, no matter how much I'd paid for products at the beauty counter.

"Johanna?" Seb called out to the woman.

The woman looked his way, and broke into a radiant smile which made her look even more beautiful. "Seb? Is that really you?" She let out a ladylike laugh, and moved towards him.

Seb met her halfway and took her into his arms.

Peggy pursed her lips, threw Seb a disgusted look, and said, "I'll get my own tea, then."

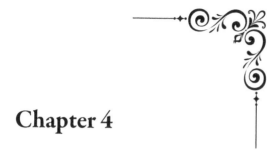

Chapter 4

My ex-husband had cheated on me constantly, and even though I knew he was doing it I'd put up with his cheating ways. Until I couldn't put up with them any longer. His cheating ways had left my heart bruised and I swore I'd never trust another man. Then Seb came back into my life. As I looked at him now, with his arms around another woman, I didn't feel the slightest twinge of jealousy. With a deep certainty, I knew Seb would never cheat on me. He glanced my way, and the love in his eyes for me confirmed my feelings.

Seb released the woman known as Johanna, and brought her over to us.

I realised Peggy, Erin and I hadn't said a single word while he'd been hugging Johanna. Which was unusual for us.

Seb said, "This is Johanna Clark. We were at university at the same time."

Johanna linked her hand through his arm. "That seems a lifetime ago. And I'm Johanna Mullen now."

"Mullen?" Seb asked. "Don't tell me you married Jerry Mullen? That poor boy was after you for years. Didn't he ask you out every day?"

"He did. And I finally said yes. Jerry and Johanna. We sound like a double act." A teasing look came into her eyes. "I was at a low point after you broke my heart. I thought I'd never recover."

"You were a couple?" Peggy asked sharply. "When? How long did it last? And how serious was it?"

"Peggy, we don't need to know that," I said politely. Then I looked at Johanna and waited for her to answer.

Erin and Peggy looked at her too.

Johanna said, "It was only for a few months. But they were intense months."

I stiffened slightly. I did not need to know that.

Seb said, "They weren't that intense. And I think it was less than two months from what I recall."

Johanna's gaze lingered too long on Seb as she said, "It was long enough to make me fall in love with you. You're an easy man to love, Seb Parker."

I heard Peggy mutter something under her breath, but thankfully, I couldn't make her words out.

Seb pulled himself free from Johanna's grip, and moved to my side. He said, "This is Karis, my..." He gave me a questioning look.

"Girlfriend," Peggy snapped. "The love of his life. His one and only."

"Yes, that's what she is," Seb said as he looked into my eyes.

Johanna said sharply, "Karis? The same Karis you used to talk about when you were drunk? The one whom you'd hurt?" She turned her smile on me. It was a smile which didn't reach her eyes. "Your name came up again and again when Seb and I were a couple. I always wondered who this woman was who had a strange hold over Seb."

"And now you've met her," Seb said. "And I thank my lucky stars every day that we're back together."

My heart went all fluttery at his words. I said to Johanna, "Are you here for the birthday party?"

"I am. Klaudia is my daughter. Believe it or not, I'm Primrose's grandma."

Peggy said, "I can believe that."

"Would you like to take a seat with the other adults?" Erin asked. "There's a fresh pot of tea on the tables at the back. If you don't want a tea, I can get you a coffee."

"Tea is fine," Johanna replied. Her gaze went to Seb. "My husband isn't able to make it to the party due to ill health. Perhaps you'd like to keep me company?"

"No, thank you. I promised Karis I'd help out with the party. And I'm not going to break any promises I make to Karis."

Johanna gave me the quickest of dismissive glances before sashaying away.

Seb smiled at me before saying to Peggy, "I'll get you your tea now. Karis, Erin, do you want anything?"

"No thanks," Erin and I replied together.

As soon as Seb disappeared into the kitchen, Erin said quietly, "Karis, if there is going to be a murder here today, I think it might be you pushing Johanna down the steps. Or the other way around."

"Murder?" Peggy asked. "What's all this about a murder. Tell me everything."

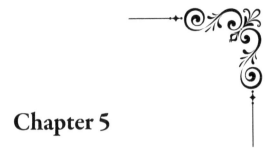

Chapter 5

I quietly told Peggy about the shadow I'd seen falling down the stairs, and that I didn't know if it was a vision from the past or the future. Or if it was a murder.

She nodded. "I'll keep an eye on the steps, and anyone who goes that way. Not that I'll be able to stop anything happening if it's meant to happen. If someone's time is up, then it's up."

"Not necessarily," I said unconvincingly.

Seb came out of the kitchen with Peggy's tea. He said, "I'll check on the adults to make sure they've got everything they need." He looked over at Robbie and smiled. "Look at him with those kids. It's like he's cast a spell on them. He's going to make a great father." He started to walk away, stopped, looked over his shoulder at Erin, and added, "And you're going to make a marvellous mum."

"Nice save," Erin told him.

Seb smiled before walking away.

Peggy nudged me, and said, "Seb will make you a wonderful husband one day, Karis."

My cheeks grew warm. "Shh. He'll hear you."

"Good. Maybe it'll give him a nudge," Peggy said. "Neither of you are getting any younger. And any fool can see he's smitten with you."

I didn't say anything because a heavily-pregnant woman and a man came over to us. Unlike my radiant sister, this woman looked exhausted as she waddled closer.

"Klaudia, hi," Erin said. "How are you feeling?"

"Don't ask," Klaudia said with a grimace. "Everything takes so much effort. And I feel so frumpy and worn out."

The man gently put his arms around her shoulders and gave her the same look which Robbie bestowed on Erin all the time. He said, "You get more beautiful every day."

Klaudia smiled at him. "You have to say that. It's part of your duties as a husband."

He kissed her on the cheek. "I'd say it even if we weren't married." He looked at me. "Hi. I'm Dean Olson. You must be Karis. Thanks so much for letting us having Primrose's party here. The café looks amazing."

"That's all down to Erin. She's organised everything."

Erin said, "Not everything. Klaudia, you mentioned an entertainer. Will they be here soon?"

"He should be." She frowned. "I'd better ring him just to be sure he's still coming."

She shuffled away. Dean kept his arm around her as if guarding a precious package.

Erin put her finger under her nose. "Karis, I have to get out of here. The smell is making me feel sick."

"The children?"

"Everything. Even the tea and coffee. I don't know what's wrong with me. It feels like my body's not my own anymore."

"Maybe the twins are getting ready to come out."

"Don't say that! I'm not ready! I haven't had the nesting instinct yet. I'm supposed to have the nesting instinct and clean my house from top to bottom. That's what it says in all the books. I haven't even put the washing in today. I refuse to have these babies until I have the nesting instinct."

I put my hands on her shoulders and gently turned her around. "Don't panic. Let's take you into the kitchen and get you away from all these unpleasant aromas."

We went into the kitchen. I was astounded once more at the amount of food Erin had prepared. I knew from past experience of children's parties that children would only eat half of the food presented to them. But I didn't tell Erin that.

I gave the rainbow unicorn cake an appreciative look. It was amazing. Almost too good to eat. I wondered if I could ask Erin to make one for me. Not for any special occasion, but just because I like cake.

Erin moved to the nearest plate of food. "I don't think there's enough food. I should make some more."

"There is more than enough." I cast a look at the overflowing trays. A particular tray caught my attention. My right hand began to tingle. I moved closer to the tray. The tingle on my palm increased.

Erin was saying something as she moved around the table, but her words sounded like a buzz in my ears.

Unable to stop myself, I reached for one of the custard tarts on the tray in front of me. I didn't have any control over my hand. I couldn't stop what was going to happen.

I lifted the tart, slowly turned around, and threw the custard tart at my pregnant sister.

The second the tart left my hand, the horror of what was happening shot through me like an arrow. I yelled, "Erin! Watch out!"

Chapter 6

Just at that moment, Seb came into the kitchen. With lightning reflexes, he leapt forward and threw himself in front of the airborne custard tart. It hit him squarely in the chest, and he stumbled backwards.

The pie slid down his shirt and fell to the floor with a squelch.

There was a stunned silence.

Then Erin cried out, "Karis! What the heck! If you don't like custard pies, then just tell me. There's no need to throw one at me."

I rushed over to her side. My hands trembled as I pulled her into a hug, which was awkward given the size of her stomach. "I'm so sorry. I don't know what came over me. Are you okay?"

"I am okay, just in shock because my sister tried to attack me." Her voice was less angry now. "Death by custard tart. That's an unusual way to go."

"I'm so sorry," I said again. "So sorry."

She patted my back, and gently pushed me away from her. "No harm done. Not to me anyway. I can't say the same for Seb."

We looked at the custard-splattered man. He was attempting to wipe the mess from his shirt with paper towels. He wasn't having any luck and was only making it worse. He said, "I've got a spare shirt in the car. I always carry spares, because you never know when you'll be the victim of a flying custard pie. Karis, why did you throw it?"

I gave him a helpless shrug. "I couldn't stop myself. It was an impulsive action, but it felt like I'd done it before many times. The sight of the pies was like a trigger."

Seb smiled pleasantly as if was an acceptable thing for me to say. "If you were aiming at Erin, you were right on target. You obviously have a hidden talent. Excuse me while I go and change."

He left the kitchen.

Erin burst out laughing. "He's so polite! Did you see the state of him?"

I tried not to smile. "He did look a mess. Poor chap." I gave Erin a concerned look. "Are you sure you're okay? I didn't mean to give you a shock. Not in your condition. You could have gone into early labour. Let me clean the floor before someone slips on it."

I made Erin sit down while I quickly cleaned the floor. As soon as I'd finished, the kitchen door opened again. It was Peggy who came in this time.

Erin said to her, "Karis just tried to kill me with a custard tart. But she got Seb instead."

Peggy frowned. "Why do I keep missing things? First, it was your vision, Karis. And now I've missed you trying to kill your sister. Can you have the decency to wait until I'm nearby before doing anything else? I'd very much appreciate that."

"I'm not doing it on purpose. And I didn't try to kill her. I was merely lobbing a custard tart at her, that's all."

Peggy tutted. "Well, that makes all the difference, doesn't it. Where's Seb? Or is he a corpse now? Have you got rid of his body?"

"He's still alive." I stopped talking as the hairs on the back of my neck lifted. "This custard tart throwing is connected to my earlier vision. I just know it is."

Erin said, "I was just thinking the same thing. You don't think the custard tarts are related to Klaudia's entertainer, do you?"

"What do you mean?" Peggy asked.

I already knew what Erin was thinking, and said, "Has she booked a clown?"

"I've no idea," Erin replied. She carefully got to her feet. "I'll ask her."

As she opened the kitchen door, a scream shot out. It was followed by a terrible noise.

The noise of someone falling down a set of stairs.

I rushed out of the kitchen and over to the steps. The safety gate was open, and a man was lying on the floor. He wasn't moving, and he was dressed as a clown.

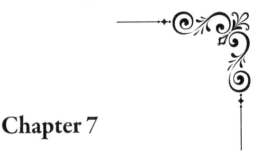

Chapter 7

A small crowd of adults had gathered around the body. Robbie must have been aware of what had happened because he was almost shouting as he tried to keep the children's attention on him.

All of a sudden, the clown leapt to his feet, and shouted, "Ta-da!" He took his hat off with a flourish and bowed.

He then proceeded to dance from side to side with a big smile on his brightly painted face.

For a moment, no one knew how to react.

There were a few uncertain claps, but not from me.

I swiftly went to the clown's side, and through clenched teeth, I hissed, "What are you playing at? There are children here. You could have scared them." I fought to keep my voice calm when all I wanted to do was shout at the thoughtless creature.

He twirled, took another bow, and said, "It's all part of the act. Feel free to applaud. I am completely unharmed."

"For now," Peggy said loudly. "You idiot! This is a children's party. What are you going to do next? Hang yourself from the ceiling?"

Through his face paint, the clown shot her a filthy look. "I would never do something so irresponsible. Throwing myself down steps is something I do regularly. I'm an expert at it. And it usually goes down a storm."

Peggy snapped, "We don't want a storm. Not when there are children about."

At that point, Klaudia and her husband came over.

"What's going on?" Dean asked. "Are you our clown? Dazzle, isn't it?"

The clown lifted his chin. "Dazzle is my name. Dazzling is my game."

Peggy jerked her thumb in Dazzle's direction. "He just threw himself down the stairs. The children could have seen him. They might have tried to copy him. You should send him packing."

Dazzle folded his arms over his red, sequined costume. "I'll still need paying."

Dean looked at his wife. "What should we do? We've paid for him. And I don't think any of the kids saw him."

Klaudia looked over at the children. A few of them were staring our way. Thankfully, the rest were still under Robbie's spell.

Klaudia said to Dazzle, "You might as well stay. But don't do anything else to scare the children."

"It's not in my nature to scare my audience. I'm in the business of dazzling. And I'm ready to dazzle! Let the show begin." He thrust his chest out, pushed his way through the crowd, and headed towards the children. His dignified exit was marred by the squeaking of his oversized shoes. Whether they squeaked by accident or design, I didn't know. And I didn't care. There was something extremely unlikeable about that clown.

The adults went back to their seats.

Erin's face was full of worry.

"What's wrong?" I asked her.

She whispered, "It's Robbie. He's terrified of clowns."

I said to Erin, "Your big strong husband who has faced the hardest of criminals in his police career is scared of clowns?"

She nodded. "The very same. There was an incident in his childhood concerning a clown. He's never given me the full details, and I haven't pushed him for them. I told him to try therapy, but he said he can't even bear to say the word clown, let alone talk about them. He said the only way to deal with his fear is to avoid clowns at all costs."

We slowly looked in Robbie's direction. I had never seen anyone look so white. His eyes were wide with terror as Dazzle performed a dance for the children inches away from him. Robbie looked frozen with fear.

"I'd better get him," Erin said.

"Do you need some help?" I asked.

"No, I'll be fine. It's not the first time we've had a clown incident. I know how to deal with this, and what to say to him."

She headed over to Robbie and took one of his hands in hers. Using her other hand, she stroked his hair and whispered something in his ear. His eyes still wide, Robbie nodded a little, and then allowed himself to be led away from the horrifying clown.

Erin took Robbie into the kitchen, still whispering to him.

Peggy said, "Now we have another reason to hate that stupid clown." She corrected herself. "Hate's too strong a word. But I don't like him one little bit. Clowns are supposed to be friendly, but he's not. I can see evil in his eyes. And listen to how he's talking to the children. So condescending. If it was up to me, I'd have told him to sling his hook by now."

I nodded in agreement. "The children seem to like him, though."

We folded our arms and gave the performer hard looks. Despite his sparkling costume, diamante bowtie and glittering shoes, he didn't dazzle us.

Seb returned to the party in a fresh shirt. He did a double-take when he saw our expressions. He asked, "Has something happened?"

Peggy informed him of the clown's antics. She said, "Can you arrest him for being an inconsiderate fool?"

"If I went around arresting people for being inconsiderate fools, the prisons would be overrun. I can glower at him if you like? Like you two are doing. Would that help?" He cast a glower at Dazzle.

" I suppose that will have to do," Peggy relented.

Dazzle continued his performance. But it wasn't long before he upset someone.

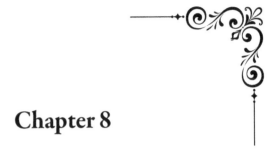

Chapter 8

The trouble started after Dazzle had performed a trick involving a wand which kept breaking whenever he tried to do magic with it. The children screamed with laughter at that. When the laughter had died down, Dazzle asked for a volunteer for his next trick.

Little hands shot up, and small bottoms wriggled excitedly on the floor as each child hoped they'd be chosen.

Even from the other side of the room, I could see an evil glint in Dazzle's eyes. What was he up to?

Dazzle said, "Where's the birthday girl? Primrose, where are you?"

A bright-eyed girl wearing a purple dress decorated with a unicorn jumped to her feet like she was on a spring. She yelled, "I'm here! I'll be the volunteer!" She ran over to Dazzle and gazed at him in utter adoration. "I'll be the volunteer."

There was a definite smirk on Dazzle's face as he continued, "That's sweet of you, princess, but my magic trick is too strong for you. Where's your dad? He can be my volunteer."

Primrose's little shoulders dropped in disappointment. She sadly pointed to her dad at the back of the room.

Dean shook his head. "No thanks. Pick someone else."

Dazzle boomed out, "Don't be shy! You don't want to let your daughter down, do you? On her special day? No father would do that to his daughter. Primrose, tell your dad to come here."

Primrose sighed dramatically as only a six-year-old could. She put her hands on her hips. "Dad. Come here. You have to do the magic."

Dean received a push from his wife before getting reluctantly to his feet. He trudged over to Dazzle, and muttered, "Make it quick."

Primrose was still standing next to the clown. Dean stood at her side. Dazzle gave them both an exaggerated look-over. His smirk increased. Loudly and clearly, he said, "Are you sure you're related? You don't look anything like each other." He looked over at Klaudia. "Is there something we should know about your window cleaner? Or a local handyman?"

My breath caught in my throat at his rude words. There was a smattering of polite laughter from the adults. Many eyes turned to Klaudia. The young woman's face was blank as she stared at Dazzle.

The horrible clown made a few more comments along the same lines, but didn't get any reaction from Klaudia. Dean had the same blank look on his face which Klaudia did. Dean didn't even look at his wife.

Dazzle hadn't finished tormenting the couple. He said to Dean, "I'm going to make you disappear. I think your wife would like that." He winked at Klaudia. "You'd like that, wouldn't you? Then you could get back to your handyman."

There wasn't any polite laughter this time. The atmosphere turned hostile.

Seb walked swiftly over to Dazzle, and stood right in front of him. He turned his back on the clown, and announced, "Children, I think it's time for food now." He shot me a questioning look. I nodded as I'd noticed Erin was starting to put food out. Seb continued talking to the children, "The food is on those tables behind you."

"I haven't finished," Dazzle said with a snarl. He attempted to push Seb out of the way, but Seb stood his ground and broke into an impromptu rendition of "Happy Birthday." Everyone soon joined in. Dazzle was the only one who wasn't singing. He was too busy giving Seb filthy looks.

As soon as the song was over, Dean took Primrose by the hand and led her over to the food table. He completely ignored his wife.

But Klaudia didn't notice because she was being comforted by another man. A dark-haired man who'd been sitting behind her. His hand was on her shoulder, and he was whispering in her ear. Klaudia's eyes were shining with tears as she nodded at whatever the man was saying. My suspicious mind looked to see if the mystery man bore any resemblance to Primrose. I couldn't tell from where I was. I noticed other people sneaking looks at him too.

Dazzle said loudly, "I guess it's time for food then. I'll be doing the second part of my act after the refreshments." He waited expectedly as if expecting applause. He didn't get any. He muttered something under his breath before walking away leaving a red sequin on the floor.

Erin came out of the kitchen holding hands with her white-faced husband. Robbie shot a nervous glance at Dazzle. The clown gave him a friendly wave which caused Robbie to tremble. Erin dragged her husband over to a corner table, and then quickly gathered a plate of food for him which she placed on his lap. Robbie nibbled on a sandwich while keeping his eyes on Dazzle. Robbie was braced as if he was ready to flee if the clown came any closer.

Pearl said, "I'll go over and give Erin a hand. She's doing far too much again, but can you tell her that? Well, I can tell her that, but does she listen? No, she doesn't." She walked over to the food tables.

Erin kissed Robbie on the cheek before heading over to the tables which were surrounded by little people. She smiled at the children, and began to help them fill their plates. Seb was already there doing the same. I noticed Johanna was at Seb's side. She was chatting to him, but Seb seemed to be only half-listening as he helped the eager children at his side. As Johanna talked, I noticed her attention kept going to someone behind me. A glance over my shoulder confirmed she was looking at Dazzle. Why was she so interested in him?

I felt a rough tap on my shoulder. It was the clown. His make-up looked even more startling close-up. He said, "Don't mind if I go into the kitchen to eat, do you? I'd rather not mix with the riff-raff during my break. And I can't be bothered with all that autograph-signing business either."

"Has anyone asked for your autograph?" I asked.

He smirked. "Not yet, but they will. They always do. Bring me a plate of food into the kitchen. I don't want any of that vegan stuff either. I want proper food."

I pointed to the table where the adults had gathered. "You can get your own food, if you don't mind mixing with the riff-raff for a little while." I gave him a pleasant smile before walking over to Erin.

Erin was smiling at a little girl. "I love your dress," Erin said. "I wish I could find a dress like that to fit me."

The little girl beamed with delight and did a little twirl. She pointed at Erin's stomach, and said, "Have you eaten too many sweets?"

Erin laughed. "I have, but I've got two babies in here."

The little girl's mouth fell open. "Two babies? In there? Are they stuck? How did they get in there?"

"Erm," Erin began. "You should ask your parents about that. Would you like another sandwich?"

"Yes, please."

Erin placed another sandwich on the small plate, and then handed it to the child.

The girl gave Erin's stomach a curious look. "How will the babies get out?"

"You should ask your parents about that too," Erin told her.

The girl nodded. "I will." She walked away with a thoughtful look on her face.

Erin grimaced. "Will I have to answer questions like that with my two?"

"Yes. How are you doing?" My voice fell to a whisper. "Is the smell overpowering still?"

She smiled. "No, it's gone away. They don't smell too bad now. I think I quite like them. Most of them anyway."

I gave her a vague nod. Something was going on behind me. Something interesting.

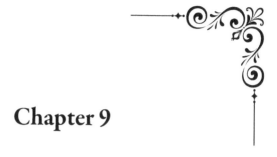

Chapter 9

Dazzle was standing at the end of the table which had been assigned to the adults. He was holding a plate piled high with food. His painted mouth was stretched into a wide smile as he looked at Dean. It was a mocking smile. Dean must have thought so too because he moved over to the clown and started to say something. I couldn't quite hear what they were talking about, so being the nosy type, I moved a bit closer until I could make out their words. And to make sure I could see their faces, I began to move some of the food plates around on the pretence of doing something.

Through clenched teeth, Dean said to the clown, "That was well out of order."

"What was?" Dazzle replied innocently.

"You know full well what."

Dazzle let out a snort. "I just said what other people are thinking. You must have thought it too. It's none of my business if you and your missus have an open marriage."

Dean's hands curled into fists. "How dare you! I should—"

"Should what?" Dazzle interrupted him. "Get your own back on your wife? Haven't you already done that?"

Dean paled. "What do you mean by that?"

"You know exactly what I mean." The glittering malice in Dazzle's eyes matched the sparkle of his twinkling outfit. He went on, "Haven't I seen you somewhere before? Visiting a certain young lady? A young lady who's nifty with her hands?"

Dean backed up. "I don't know who you're talking about."

"Of course you don't." Dazzle tapped the side of his red nose. "Let's keep this to ourselves. We don't want to upset your wife, not in her delicate condition." He glanced to the side. "Although, she doesn't look upset at the moment. Who is that man who's comforting her?"

I looked that way too. The same man who'd been whispering to Klaudia earlier now had his arm around her shoulders. His other hand was resting gently on her distended tummy in an intimate gesture.

Dean muttered something under his breath before rushing over to his wife. As soon as they saw him approaching, Klaudia and the mystery man sprang apart.

Dazzle chuckled, and then picked a cupcake up and headed to the kitchen.

As soon as he'd gone through the kitchen door, Johanna followed him. She had a strange look on her face. A mixture of anger and fear. Was she going to confront Dazzle about his cruel comments? I didn't know whether I should follow them. Perhaps I could hover near the door to make sure things didn't get out of hand.

A voice broke into my thoughts. "Well then? Is there going to be a murder or not?"

It was Peggy.

I took her over to one side. "I'm not sure, but I know Dazzle has upset Dean." I told her what I'd overheard, and about Johanna going into the kitchen after the clown.

Peggy nodded towards the kitchen. "She's coming back out now. Looking all flushed too. I wonder what she's been up to."

I looked at Johanna. Her cheeks were red, and her eyes were too bright as if she was about to cry. She was rubbing her cheek with a tissue.

Peggy said, "Do you think they've been canoodling in there? She might be wiping his face paint off her cheek."

"You've got a suspicious mind, Peggy."

"I know. Were you thinking the same thing?"

I nodded. "I've got an awful feeling something dreadful is going to happen soon. I'm going to look at the stairs again and see if that shadow appears."

"I'll come with you." Peggy cast a look around the café. "Everything seems in order here. Seb is doing a marvellous job. Which is just as well because Robbie is about as much use as a chocolate teapot at the moment."

"He's scared of clowns," I explained.

Peggy let out a dismissive sniff. "That's no excuse. I'm scared of spiders, but I don't let the little blighters stop me living my life. If he doesn't sort himself out soon, I'll be having a word with him. He can't expect Erin to do everything."

I felt a rush of sympathy for Robbie. I think he must have picked up on Peggy's intention because he looked her way, swallowed nervously and got to his feet. He walked over to Erin and helped her collect some empty plates.

Peggy and I headed to the stairs. The safety gate was closed. We stared silently at the steps.

I waited, but I didn't get a premonition.

"Well?" Peggy asked. "Anything?"

"No, but maybe the shadow I saw earlier was Dazzle throwing himself down the stairs on purpose."

Peggy nodded. "I hope so. Maybe you weren't witnessing a possible murder after all."

I held my hand up. I could see something happening at the top of the stairs. An indistinct shadow slowly appeared. It moved towards the top step and took shape. It looked male. And he was wearing oversized shoes. Like a clown.

The clown shadow held his hands out as if presenting himself to an audience. He took a bow, and I heard a low rumble of applause floating in the air.

Taking a step down, the shadow waved at the invisible audience. I could still hear the applause coming from an unseen audience.

As the clown reached the third step, I forgot to breathe because I knew what was going to happen next.

And it did.

The clown tumbled down the steps. The applause continued, but as the shadow lay unmoving at the bottom of the stairs, the applause died down to be replaced with cries of horror.

I stared at the shadowy figure at my feet. I caught a twinkle of a red sequin before the shadow melted away.

I blinked, looked at Peggy, and said, "It isn't over yet."

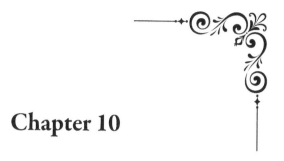

Chapter 10

There was a commotion in the main area of the café.

"What's going on?" Peggy asked as she rushed away.

I went after her expecting to see something awful.

But the commotion was just the noise of restless children who'd eaten too much sugar and wanted to let off steam. Bits of discarded food littered the floor. A couple of boys were flinging themselves across the floor on their knees. It was a mystery to me as to why they did that. Groups of girls were pulling down some of the unicorn posters from the walls. A couple of children had decided to race around the café.

Someone let out a sharp whistle causing the children to come to a sudden stop. It was Seb. He held his hands up, and using his official police voice, said, "That's enough. Move to the front area, sit down, and place a finger on your lips."

Such was the authority in his voice, that the children immediately obeyed. Some of the adults moved towards the front too before realising Seb was only talking to the children.

Peggy said quietly, "He looks quite handsome when he gets all official, doesn't he? No wonder you love him so much."

"I don't love him," I replied.

"Of course you do. It's written all over your face." She looked left and right. "Where's that stupid clown gone? He should be out here entertaining the children." She stopped talking, and turned her worried face to me. "Unless he's dead. Didn't he go into the kitchen earlier?"

We spun around and rushed towards the kitchen.

We almost collided with Dazzle as he came out eating a sausage roll.

The clown paid us no attention as he made his way over to the seated children. Once there, he held his hands out, and announced cheerfully, "Kids! I'm back. Are you ready for more dazzling magic?"

The little ones cheered. The adults didn't. Some of them were looking at their phones.

I saw Erin tidying the mess up on the tables. Peggy and I immediately went over and assisted her.

Peggy tutted at the sight of the tables. "I don't know who's made the most mess, the adults or the children. Erin, go and have a sit-down."

"I don't want to. I'm full of energy still." She smiled as she collected some plates.

"Where's that useless husband of yours?" Peggy asked. "He should be doing this."

Erin turned to Peggy. "He's not useless. He's in the kitchen putting the finishing touches to the birthday cake."

"I thought it was already finished," I said. "It looked perfect to me."

"Not perfect enough," Erin said. "I just wanted a few more sparkling things on it. Robbie offered to do it for me. And there are some party bags to sort out too. Klaudia was going to do them at home, but she didn't get round to it."

Dazzle began his second performance. I was too busy clearing up to see what he was doing. Going by the sounds coming from the children, he was doing something amazing.

I noticed Klaudia and Dean going in and out of the kitchen at various times. Robbie popped out now and again to check on Erin. He studiously kept his eyes from looking in Dazzle's direction.

We finished cleaning up just as Dazzle came to the end of his performance. The children cheered and yelled. Dazzle bowed several times before walking away. He took something from his pocket and headed towards the adults. He started to hand out small cards which

I assumed were his business cards. Some of the adults refused to take them. The mystery man who'd been talking to Klaudia earlier was sitting three chairs away from her now. Dean was nowhere in sight.

With a flamboyant goodbye wave, Dazzle went into the kitchen. Chatter broke out amongst the adults. Seb moved over to the children, and told them to return to their parents in an orderly fashion. Which they did do. Seb looked my way and gave me a wink.

Primrose leaned against her mum, looking tired but happy. Klaudia stroked her hair and smiled lovingly at her little girl. I felt tears come to my eyes as I recalled the many happy mother-daughter moments I'd spent with my daughter, Lorrie. She was in her twenties now, but she'd always be my little girl. I made a mental note to phone her later and tell her how much I loved her.

Before I could do either, I felt a weird sensation on the back of my neck, like a cold draught.

Primrose said to her mum, "Can we go home now? I'm tired."

"I'm tired too, my little love," Klaudia replied. "But we can't go home until we've had cake. Shall we do that now?"

Primrose's face lit up. "Yes! Cake! Yes!"

Klaudia let out a groan as she heaved herself up.

Erin waddled over to her, and said, "You stay where you are. I'll bring the cake in."

The cold draught across my neck suddenly turned into an icy breeze. I shivered. I didn't need a psychic vision to tell me something horrifying had happened.

With surprising speed for a heavily pregnant woman, Erin hurried past me and into the kitchen.

I gave Peggy a pointed look, and we rushed after her.

And there he was.

Dead.

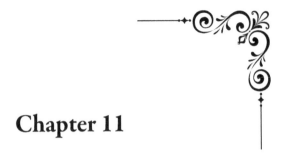

Chapter 11

Dazzle wasn't going to dazzle anyone anymore.

He was leaning over the table, and was face down in Erin's beautiful unicorn cake, his arms splayed on the table.

Peggy, Erin and I looked at the unmoving body for a few seconds. Then I quickly moved over to him and checked for a pulse. There wasn't one.

Peggy asked, "Is he...?"

I nodded. "Dead? Yes."

"Right," Peggy said. "Right. What shall we do? This is terrible."

Erin held her hands up. "Don't panic. I've got a spare cake in the fridge. I made it just in case the first one wasn't big enough. It's not quite as elaborate."

"Never mind the cake! What about him?" I pointed to the deceased clown. "We have to do something about him."

"I know, but I still have to take a birthday cake out." Erin looked closer at Dazzle's face. "Where do you think the unicorn's horn has gone? Or don't I want to know the answer to that?"

Peggy took control of the situation. "I'll stay here with the dead clown. Erin, you take the cake out and act like everything is okay. Karis, get your boyfriend in here. I'll guard the door to make sure no one comes in."

Erin nodded. She opened the fridge and took out a cake which had a smaller unicorn on the top. I held the kitchen door open while she went through. She managed to put a big smile on her face as if finding a corpse in the kitchen was nothing to worry about.

Seb was at the far side of the room. Johanna was talking animatedly to him. One of her hands was resting lightly on his arm. Seb smiled as he listened to whatever she was staying. I didn't know whether it was an interested smile or a polite one.

As I walked towards them, I considered what I should stay to Seb to alert him to the deceased entertainer.

As it turned out, I didn't have to say anything. He looked my way, locked eyes with me, and gave me a small nod. He excused himself from Johanna, and came swiftly to my side.

"Has something happened?" he whispered.

I nodded, but didn't explain.

Peggy was standing at the kitchen door with her arms folded and a grim look on her face. Like a sombre-faced bouncer, she stood to one side to let us enter.

Once inside the kitchen, it took Seb two seconds to take in what had happened. He turned to me, took me into a hug, and said, "I'll take over now. Are you okay?"

"I am," I said into his chest. I reluctantly moved out of his embrace. "Seb, I don't think this is going to be the only murder."

"What do you mean?"

"I saw the shadow on the steps again. It looked like a clown this time. And he fell down the stairs to his death." I looked towards Dazzle. "It can't be him because he didn't die on the stairs, so who else is going to die?"

"Are you sure the shadowy clown died?"

I thought about that. "No, I don't know for certain."

"Okay. That shadowy clown could have something to do with Dazzle's death and not be a premonition for a future death." He gave me a tight-lipped smile. "That could be possible, couldn't it?"

"I suppose."

"Let's deal with one murder at a time."

Chapter 12

Some hours later, we were gathered at Erin's house. The party guests had left the café without knowing about the tragedy. Klaudia had wanted to say goodbye to Dazzle, but I'd told her he'd already left. She said she'd contact him later to say thank you for entertaining the children so well. I smiled politely at that, but didn't say anything.

Within minutes of the last guest leaving, the police arrived at the back door. Seb came out of the kitchen and had a quick chat with us.

He looked at Erin who was sitting at a table and staring at the floor. He said to me, "Take Erin home. She looks pale."

"I will do, but then I'm coming back. I have to tidy the café. I can't leave it like this. It has to be ready for tomorrow morning. Monday is our busiest day."

Seb gave me a long look before saying, "You might not be opening tomorrow. The café is now a crime scene. We might even need to close it for a few days."

"Oh. I see." I watched Robbie go over to Erin and sit at her side. He took one of her hands in his, brought it to his lips and gave it a gentle kiss. Erin smiled at him.

Peggy suddenly appeared at our side. She had her tartan coat on. "Well?" she asked Seb. "What's going on? What have you found out so far? And don't give me any of that nonsense about police privacy. We're practically family now. Tell us everything."

Seb looked as if he weren't going to say anything, but a look at Peggy's expression made him change his mind. He said, "We're still at the early stages of our investigation, but it looks like Dazzle's death could have been accidental."

"Accidental!" Peggy cried out. "Did he accidentally trip, fall on that cake and suffocate? What are you going on about?"

Seb remained polite. "If you'll give me a moment to explain, the back door has been forced open. We're dusting it for fingerprints. Mr Peel could have—"

"Who the heck is Mr Peel?" Peggy interrupted him.

"It's Dazzle's real name," Seb explained. "Alvin Peel."

Peggy said, "Alvin Peel? That's a bit disappointing. I was expecting something more showbiz. Karis, don't you think that's a poor name for a clown? Alvin Peel sounds more like an insurance salesman."

I shrugged. "I don't know. I suppose clowns are just ordinary people with everyday names."

"How do you think they choose their clown names?" Peggy asked with a thoughtful expression on her face. "What would my clown name be?"

Seb coughed politely. "If I may continue?"

"You may," Peggy told him.

Seb continued, "Mr Peel could have disturbed the intruder, and it could have turned nasty between them. There could have been a scuffle which resulted in Mr Peel falling on the cake. Unfortunately, it appears he fell right onto the unicorn horn which then choked him."

Peggy let out a sigh. "Death by unicorn. That's not something you hear every day. Will that go on his death certificate?"

"I've no idea," Seb replied. "Karis, Peggy, can you leave now, please? I really think Erin needs to go home. Robbie has already agreed to stay and help us. He'll lock up too."

I was touched about his concern over Erin, and as I looked at my sister, I realised he was right.

Even though she protested, Peggy and I got Erin into my car and drove her home. She looked even paler by the time we reached her house. She didn't argue at all as we helped her upstairs and into bed. Peggy tucked the blankets around Erin, kissed her on the forehead, and told her she loved her.

I closed the curtains, and then kissed Erin too. I said, "You get some rest. You need it. I've put your phone on the table there. Text me if you need anything. I'll be downstairs."

"And so will I," Peggy said.

Erin said feebly, "You don't have to stay. I'll be fine. Robbie will be home soon."

"We're not going anywhere," Peggy told her in a firm tone. "I'll check on you in a little while."

We left the room leaving the door ajar before Erin could argue. Not that she looked as if she had any energy to do so.

Once downstairs, we headed into the kitchen. I made cups of tea and brought them over to the table where Peggy was sitting with a thoughtful look on her face.

"What's going on in your head?" I asked her. I handed her a cup.

She cradled her hands around the cup. "I don't think that clown was killed by accident. I think he was murdered. And I'll tell you why."

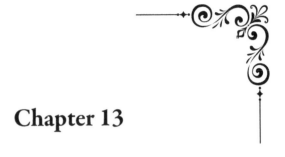

Chapter 13

Peggy began. "You heard what that nasty clown said to Dean about Primrose not being his daughter. And going by the look on Dean's face, I think he already knows that. And did you see how Klaudia studiously ignored Dean after the clown said that to him? She must know that he knows. And who was that dark-haired man who was too familiar with Klaudia? What's his part in this puzzle? Is he Primrose's real dad? And is he the father of Klaudia's unborn child?"

"That's a lot of questions, but what have they got to do with Dazzle?"

"I'm getting to that. Dean and Klaudia were in and out of the kitchen during Dazzle's second act. Was one of them still in there when Dazzle went in? Did they confront him, and that confrontation led to an argument?"

I frowned. "I can see how Dean could have pushed Dazzle onto the fatal unicorn horn, but you saw how exhausted Klaudia was. I doubt she'd have the strength to do that."

"I don't know. If she was trying to keep Primrose's parentage a secret, she could have found the strength. You know what mums are capable of when it comes to protecting their children."

I nodded. "That's true. And I suppose once Dazzle had choked on the unicorn horn, then he wouldn't have put up much of a fight to whoever was pressing him down." I drummed my fingers on the table as an image of the birthday cake came to my mind. "What was the horn made of anyway? Fondant? Or had Erin covered something conical in icing? Like a metal tube or something? That would have choked him straight away, I imagine."

"It's a possibility," Peggy agreed. "I think there was an episode of Bake Off where someone made a unicorn cake. I can't remember how they did it now." She gave a dismissive wave. "Not that it matters now. Seb can tell us later what it was made of. The point is, it wouldn't have taken a lot of force to kill Dazzle, would it?"

"I suppose not. And whoever did it, must have made the back door look as if it had been forced open." Peggy took a sip of her tea while giving me a calculating look. She put her cup down, and said, "What do you think about Johanna?"

I shifted in my seat. "In what way? She seems nice enough."

"She didn't seem nice at all to me. She had her hands all over Seb. And she didn't pay her granddaughter any attention. She positively recoiled when Primrose came up to her. I caught her looking at Dazzle a few times from the start of the party like she knew him. And don't forget her little trip into the kitchen when he was in there. She could have sneaked into the kitchen later after his second act."

"Why would she kill him?"

"To protect her daughter's reputation? Or maybe he's an old boyfriend and he made a pass at her? And don't forget the mystery man who had his hands on Klaudia. He could have killed Dazzle too."

I put my hands around my cup. "Yes, any of them could have done it. But there's one problem. They all have the same motive of protecting Klaudia. But don't forget about my vision. Why did I see that shadow of a clown falling down the stairs? It's got something to do with Dazzle, I just know it has."

Peggy gave me a slow nod. "Yes, but what? I think we should make some investigations of our own. If Seb thinks it was an accident, then he won't take Dazzle's death any further, will he?"

"I'm not sure, Peggy. We should wait to see what Seb finds out. We shouldn't interfere."

Peggy let out a sound which sounded suspiciously like a cackle. "We never interfere. We just assist the police with their enquiries."

"Even when they don't ask us to?" I asked with a smile.

The noise which came from Peggy now was most definitely a cackle. "Especially when they don't ask for it. Let me check on Erin, and then we'll make a plan of action."

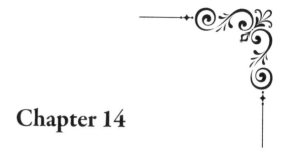

Chapter 14

O nce I'd had a good night's sleep, I decided we shouldn't proceed with Peggy's plan of action which involved talking to Klaudia, Dean, Johanna, and the mystery man. Peggy said she'd interrogate them until they cracked under pressure and admitted the truth to us. We were at Peggy's house when she concocted the plan, and she was on her second gin and tonic when she was putting the finer parts of her plan together.

I kept telling her to leave the investigation to Seb, but she was already on a mission to find out who'd killed Dazzle, and I don't think an express train would have stopped her.

Seb had phoned me late the previous night to say the café could open as normal the following day. I didn't tell him about Peggy's plans, and he didn't tell me anything about Alvin Peel's death. Even though I wanted to know, I didn't push him. If he wanted me to know anything, then he'd tell me.

So, on Monday morning, I opened the café bright and early. I felt a bit queasy going into the kitchen, but it had to be done. I steeled myself before I entered it, but was relieved to see the kitchen was tidy and spotless. I half expected to see a chalk outline of the deceased clown. Did the police even do that anymore?

Even though the kitchen was clean, I still shivered. If Dazzle had been murdered, what was the reason for it? And what did his death have to do with that shadow on the stairs?

I shook my head at myself. I was going to let the police deal with everything. I had other things on my mind, and my sister was right at the front of the queue. Peggy and I hadn't left Erin's house the previous evening until Robbie had returned home. Erin was still fast asleep so we didn't disturb her before we left.

I had phoned her this morning and told her firmly not to come to the café. To my surprise, my stubborn sister had immediately agreed. That had worried me, and I had to refrain myself from driving round to her house to check on her. But I sent her a few text messages instead, and she had replied with short answers, which wasn't like her either.

I set up the café for the day. The staff arrived soon after. I felt it only right to tell them about Dazzle dying in the kitchen. They were shocked but remained professional as they went about their duties.

We were soon busy, and I didn't have time to text Erin. She was constantly on my mind, though.

Our café is on two floors with the upper level being a quieter area. It was normal for me to go up and down the stairs many times a day to serve the customers up there. As I came back down on one of those trips , I saw Jen waiting for me at the bottom of the stairs. Jen had worked for us a while, and she was one of those wonderful people who would do anything for anyone.

When I saw her concerned face, I immediately asked, "What's wrong? Is it Erin?"

She shook her head. "It's you."

"Me? Why?"

She pointed to the stairs. "Every time you go up and down these steps, you miss the third stair from the top out. You take a double step to avoid it. Both coming up, and going down."

"Do I?" I hadn't even noticed.

"Yes. Is there something wrong with that step?"

I glanced at the offending step. It looked like all the others. "There's nothing wrong with it." Jen knew about my psychic abilities, so I took her into my confidence and told her about my vision.

She said, "You have to do something about this. You're going to slip on the steps if you're not careful."

I gave her a helpless shrug. "The police are dealing with the clown's death."

"That's not good enough. You could fall to your death before they decide if that clown was murdered or not. Can't you do something? If you're avoiding that step, doesn't that mean there's something for you to do?"

"You sound like Peggy," I said with a small smile.

"Did someone mention my name?"

Like a genie in a tartan coat, Peggy appeared behind us.

Before I could say a word, Jen jerked her thumb at the steps and said, "Karis is going to break her neck on these stairs if she doesn't do something about her latest vision."

Peggy asked for clarification, and when she got it, she said to me, "Get your coat. We're going out. Your life is in danger, and we're going to do something about it."

"My life is hardly in danger," I pointed out.

Jen and Peggy folded their arms at the same time, and gave me the same hard look which made me back up a little.

Peggy repeated, "Get your coat. I know where we're going first."

There was no arguing with her, so I got my coat.

Chapter 15

Before I switched the engine on, I asked Peggy where we were going.

"To see Klaudia. I've got a receipt to give her, to confirm the party invoice has been paid."

I threw her a confused look before starting the car and setting off. "We don't give printed receipts. Everything is online."

Peggy pulled her handbag closer to her. "Klaudia doesn't know that. And anyway, it would be courteous of us to call on her considering what has happened. You know, with the dead clown."

"Does she know about him? I don't want to bring the subject up if she doesn't know."

"She does know. I spoke to Seb this morning and asked him. I didn't tell him we're going to make our own enquiries because he doesn't need to know that. He's spoken to Dean and Johanna too. He wouldn't tell me what they said which I thought was very rude. He wouldn't even tell me whether he still thought Dazzle's death was an accident or not. I was very disappointed with our conversation."

I smiled at her words. "Where does Klaudia live?"

She gave me the directions, and we headed that way.

I said, "I do like the idea of checking on Klaudia. She was upset yesterday about what Dazzle said during his act. She must be feeling even worse today knowing that he's dead."

"Unless she's the one who killed him. Then she'll be worried the police are on to her. She might have even done a runner."

"I don't think she'll get very far in her condition."

Peggy said, "Never underestimate a pregnant woman. Or any woman come to that."

I nodded. "That's very true."

We drove on in silence for a bit.

All of a sudden, Peggy yelled, "Go that way! To the right. Follow that van!"

"What? Where? Who?" I slowed down.

"It's Dean Olson driving that van. It says his name on the side of it, along with him being a painter and decorator. Karis, turn right. Don't let him get away."

I turned right. "Why are we following him?"

"He looked shifty. He's up to something."

"You can't follow a person just because they look shifty," I said. But I followed the van anyway as it turned left.

"I want to see where he's going. Remember what Dazzle said yesterday about Dean seeing another woman? He might be on his way to see her right now. Why else would he look shifty? And he's on our list of suspects anyway. We were going to talk to him at some point."

"Were we?"

"Yes. Look, he's slowing down. Keep your distance. Don't let him know we're following him."

The white van came to a stop outside a neat-looking semi-detached house. We parked a little way down the road, but not too far because we wanted to see what was going on.

Dean got out of his van and went to the rear doors of it. He opened them, and took out a bag which was overflowing with rolls of wallpaper. He locked the van, and then walked towards the house.

I said to Peggy, "It looks like he's doing a decorating job. I don't think he's here for anything other than work."

"Just hold your horses there, Karis. Look at how he's grinning. It's a grin full of mischief and guilt. Let's watch what he does next."

The front door of the house opened, and a woman wearing a tight-fitting dress stood there. She looked left and right before grinning at Dean. She put her hand on her hip and gave him a flirtatious look. Dean almost broke into a sprint as he hurried down the path and into the house. Before the door closed we saw the coupe embrace.

Peggy and I stared silently at the house. My heart was racing too fast as memories of my ex-husband's betrayals flooded my mind. I thought I was over the hurt by now, but obviously not. I didn't have any feelings for my ex, but that didn't stop the pain.

"What a cad," Peggy said dryly. "And that's not the word I want to use. Karis, you'd better drive us away before I rush over to that house, and drag that horrible man out of there."

She didn't need to tell me twice. My tyres squealed as I drove away from Dean Olson and the woman he was having an affair with.

Chapter 16

The last person I wanted to see was the pregnant woman whose husband was cheating on her. But, there was a murder to solve, and I wouldn't get any peace until the murderer was brought to justice.

Peggy was silent as we drove along, but her disgusted face gave her feelings away.

When we pulled up outside Klaudia's house, Peggy said, "You don't have to come in and talk to Klaudia. I can see how upset you are. This must be bringing up lots of bad memories about that awful ex-husband of yours. I can talk to her on my own."

I released my seat belt. "I'll be fine. I want to see her reaction when we talk about Dazzle." I paused. "Do you think she knows about Dean and his other woman?"

"Maybe. But as annoyed as I am with Dean, I'm not going to be the one to tell her if she doesn't know."

"Me neither. Even though I'm tempted to do so. It isn't fair that she doesn't know."

When Klaudia opened her door to us, I couldn't help but take a sharp intake of breath. The young woman looked dead on her feet. Her face was pale, and there were dark circles under her eyes. She looked as if she hadn't slept for days. It could have been part of her pregnancy, or something else.

She gave us a wan smile, and said, "Are you here about Dazzle? That poor man. I can't believe he's dead, and how he died. I'm so sorry it happened in your lovely café. I feel so responsible."

"It's not your fault," I said, but part of me wondered if it was her fault that Dazzle was dead. "I hope it hasn't spoiled the party for you."

She ran her hand over her swollen stomach. "Dazzle spoiled the party for me before he died. Would you like to come in? I could do with some company. I'll put the kettle on."

We went into her house. I noticed how Klaudia winced with pain as she led us into the living room. Toy boxes were placed optimistically along the sides of the room, but the boxes were empty. Their contents were strewn haphazardly around the room. It was like tackling an obstacle course as we carefully made our way through the debris and over to the sofa.

Klaudia waved a tired hand at the toys. "Sorry about the mess. I keep tidying it up, and before I know it, the mess is back. Would you like a tea or coffee?"

Peggy said, "I'll make them. Sit yourself down, Klaudia. Have you eaten today? Can I make you something to eat?"

"I haven't had anything yet. I feel a bit queasy over the dying clown business. Primrose wants to send a thank you card to him. That was the last thing she said to me when I dropped her off at school this morning. I just gave her a nod. How can I tell her he's dead?"

I said, "You don't have to tell her." Worried that she might trip over a stray toy, I took her gently by the elbow as she came closer. I put a couple of cushions in place on the sofa for her back, and then helped her to sit down.

She lowered herself on the sofa with a little groan.

Peggy took our hot drinks order, and then left the room.

My attention went to the toys. I was itching to tidy them away, but I didn't want to insult Klaudia. But then a glance at her tired face made me decide to insult her anyway.

I gently asked, "Would you mind if I tidied up a little? I don't want you tripping over anything."

Tears sprang to her eyes. "Normally, I'd be stubborn and say no, but I really would like that. Thank you so much."

"That's okay." I proceeded to put toys into boxes, at the same time chatting to Klaudia about pregnancy issues and the birth of her next child. I was pleased to see the colour come back into her face as she talked about her family, and how excited Primrose was about her new brother or sister.

Peggy came into the room carrying a tray. She placed it on the low table in front of the sofa, and said, "Klaudia, I hope you don't mind, but I've made you a couple of slices of toast to go with your tea. You need to take care of yourself." She handed a plate and a cup to Klaudia.

Klaudia gave her a grateful smile. "You are so kind. Thank you. I'm not sure I can eat much, but I'll give it a go." She stopped talking, and gave Peggy a curious look. "Are you here to talk about Dazzle? Or is there another reason why you're here? Dean paid for the party, didn't he? I told him to pay you online. I hope he didn't forget. He's been so busy with his work lately. He's hardly ever at home."

I froze at her comments about her husband. Luckily, Peggy didn't, and confirmed the party had been paid for.

Peggy added, "We wanted to make sure you were okay after hearing about Dazzle. It was quite a shock."

Klaudia took a nibble of her toast before answering, "That's kind of you to be concerned. Dean offered to stay home with me today, but I told him he should go to work. He runs his own painting and decorating business."

Foolishly, before I could stop myself, I said, "Yes, we saw his van on the way over here." As soon as the words were out, I clamped my mouth shut.

There was a sudden heavy silence. I stared intently at my cup wishing I could rewind time.

A heavy sigh came from Klaudia. I looked her way. She put her plate of toast down, and said, "Tell me."

"Tell you what?" I asked feebly. I knew exactly what she meant.

Peggy was giving Klaudia a purposely blank look.

Klaudia said, "I know you know something about Dean, but you're too polite to say anything." When we didn't speak, she continued, "Okay, let me ask you something. Where did you see Dean's van?"

"Just on the road," I answered. Klaudia's look was intense, and I added, "Near Cromer Street."

She asked, "Near Cromer Street or outside a particular house on that street?"

Her tone was so commanding that I couldn't argue with her. I replied, "It was outside a certain house on Cromer Street."

Klaudia nodded. "That'll be Kiki Robert's house. Dean's having an affair with her. I've known about it for months." She took a sip of her tea. "This is a lovely cup of tea."

I shared a shocked look with Peggy. I didn't know what to say. Although, considering my history with my ex, I wasn't shocked that Klaudia knew about her cheating husband.

Peggy wasn't silent for long. She burst out, "How can you put up with him? And in your condition too? You should fling him out on his ear!"

Klaudia's reply was a shrug.

Peggy sat forward on her chair. "You should pack his suitcase and have it ready for him on the doorstep when he comes home. I'll help you pack it, if you like. Don't let him treat you like this. It's not right."

Klaudia attempted to smile at us. "It's okay. Really. I know his affair doesn't mean anything. He loves me. He's a great husband, and he adores Primrose." Despite her words, there was hurt in her eyes. She continued quietly, "I don't want to talk about Dean anymore."

I didn't want to talk about him either. I changed the subject, and asked, "How did you find out about Dazzle's work as a party entertainer? Did someone recommend him?"

"Yes, it was Dean." She frowned. "I don't know where he got Dazzle's name from."

I said, "Perhaps Dazzle was one of his customers." I thought about the comments Dazzle had made about Dean knowing a certain woman. Were they talking about Kiki Roberts?

As if reading my mind, Klaudia said, "They probably both know Dean's mistress. I understand she's friendly with a lot of men. Perhaps she recommended him to Dean." She put her cup down. "I think I need a lie-down. I'm exhausted. Thank you for coming to see me."

We knew when we were being dismissed. Even though I had more questions for Klaudia, I was not prepared to upset her any further.

Despite Klaudia's objections, Peggy collected our cups and Klaudia's plate, took them through to the kitchen, and washed them. For my part, I helped Klaudia to her feet which almost made me topple onto the sofa. Once she was upright, we had a polite chat about Primrose's school, and how well she was doing.

As we drove away from Klaudia's house, Peggy said, "That poor woman. I don't know how she puts up with a husband like that, especially not when she's so heavily pregnant. Hasn't that man got any sense of decency?"

"He might not be the only one having an affair. You saw how close that dark-haired man was to Klaudia at the party. Perhaps she's having an affair of her own."

"Perhaps. Her mother is certainly the flirty type." Peggy shook her head. "I don't understand why people would stay together if they're both having affairs."

"Perhaps love keeps Dean and Klaudia together," I ventured. "I wonder if their confusing love lives led to the death of Dazzle somehow."

"I was thinking the same thing. How do you feel about talking to Kiki Roberts? We can find out if she knew the cruel clown."

I nodded. "I can do that. Shall we go now?"

"No time like the present."

I changed direction, and said, "We'll have to try our best to not judge Kiki."

"Too late. I've already judged her, and my opinion of her is very low," Peggy said with a dismissive sniff.

I had judged Kiki too, but I changed my mind when we met the woman a short while later.

Chapter 17

Thankfully, Dean's van had gone from outside Kiki's house when we arrived. I was grateful for that, but Peggy wasn't.

She said, "I wish that good-for-nothing was still here. I'd give him a piece of my mind."

"I'm sure you would." I switched the engine off, and turned in my seat so I could face Peggy better. "What are we going to say to her? Do we mention Dean, and that we know they're seeing each other? It's none of our business."

"It could be our business if it's related to the murder. Let me think of something on the way up the path. I'll be subtle."

Peggy was as subtle as a house brick being launched at a glasshouse. As soon as Kiki opened the door, Peggy jabbed her finger at the woman and said, "How dare you have an affair with a married man? A married man with a pregnant wife and a young daughter. You should feel ashamed of yourself."

Kiki's eyes suddenly became too bright. As I looked at her, I became aware of a dense loneliness surrounding her; it was like a heavy blanket of isolation. I felt like I could almost touch it.

In a desolate tone, Kiki said, "You can't possibly imagine how much shame I feel. I know about Dean's family, but it hasn't stopped me. I'm a terrible person. I hate myself."

Her confession took the wind from Peggy's sails, and she lowered her hand.

Some instinct made me rush forward and take Kiki in my arms. She dissolved into tears. I felt my eyes brimming with tears too. Holding her so close made my heart feel heavy as if I were absorbing her melancholy.

A minute later, and without saying anything, I released Kiki, and we went inside her house.

When we were settled in the front room, Kiki attempted to explain herself. "I didn't mean to start an affair with Dean. He came here to do some decorating work. It was just after I'd split up with my long-term boyfriend. I was feeling low and vulnerable. I know that's no excuse, but the attention Dean gave me went straight to my head."

"I see," Peggy said. It was obvious she didn't.

Kiki carried on, "I tried to end the affair, but Dean makes me feel so special. And sometimes, you just need to feel that. No matter how wrong it is." She looked at her hands as she twisted them nervously on her lap. "This is no excuse either, but he said his wife had been cheating on him for years. He suspected his daughter wasn't his, or the baby which is on the way either."

I asked, "Did he say who he thought the father was?"

She looked up from her lap. "Some old boyfriend of his wife's who'd come back on the scene. He didn't give me a name. Dean said he couldn't leave his wife because he loved her so much. And he loves Primrose as if she were his own. That's what he told me, anyway."

Like Klaudia earlier, I didn't want to talk about Dean any longer. I asked Kiki, "Do you know about the birthday party Primrose had yesterday?"

"I do. And I know about the clown dying. I feel responsible about that."

"Why?" Peggy asked sharply. "Did you know him?"

"I did. I've known him for years. Over five years, I think." Colour came to her cheeks. "We did have a fling when we first met. Once again,

I was getting over the break-up of a relationship. Even though Alvin —
that's the clown's name — was years older than me, I fell for his charms."

I pulled a face at those words. Alvin hadn't been at all charming in
my opinion. Quite the opposite.

Peggy said, "Tell us more about Alvin. Did he have any enemies? I
bet he had loads."

Kiki frowned. "It's funny you should say that. When I first met
Alvin, he had a different clown name. He was called Gloomy. That
name had been handed down through his family for generations.
Apparently, it's a clown thing to hand a name down, along with the face
make-up which is unique to each family. Did you know clowns have to
register their face make-up to stop someone else using it?"

Peggy nodded. "I saw that on a quiz show once. When did Alvin
change his clown name?"

"About a year ago." She moved over to a cupboard and opened a
drawer. She took a catalogue out and handed it to Peggy. I shuffled
closer so I could see the catalogue better. It showed pictures of clowns
in very bright costumes. Peggy flicked through the book. Many clowns
grinned brightly out at us from the pages.

Peggy said to me, "Robbie would lose his marbles if he saw this
many clowns." She gave Kiki a long look. "Why have you got a book
full of clowns? I hope it's not a fetish of some sort."

Kiki smiled at that. "I've only been seduced by one clown. I'm a
seamstress by trade. I make costumes for clowns. That's how I came to
meet Alvin. It's a surprisingly lucrative business. Clowns damage their
costumes all the time due to the nature of their business. Even the
retired ones like to have new costumes made often. It makes them feel
youthful again."

"Retired clowns?" I asked.

"Yes. Although, they don't like to refer to themselves as retired.
They say they've put their custard pies down, which I think is a lovely
expression. I actually met Alvin at the clown retirement home when

he was visiting his dad. I knew his dad well." She noticed Peggy's expression, and quickly added, "Not in that way. Alvin used to visit his dad every other week. His dad passed away about a year ago. Oh. I wonder if that's why Alvin changed his clown name from Gloomy to Dazzle around that time."

I said, "Did the name Dazzle belong to another clown?"

Kiki considered the matter. "I don't know. I shouldn't think so because it would be classed as theft, according to the clown community anyway. You should hear some of the tales they tell me about what goes on in the world of clowns."

A thought was blooming in my mind. "If the name Dazzle belonged to another clown, he wouldn't have been happy about Alvin stealing his name."

"And identity. Alvin changed his make-up and outfit too. When he was called Gloomy, he wore grey clothes. And his make-up matched his name. His mouth was always painted downwards. And no, another clown wouldn't have been happy about someone stealing his name and identity."

Peggy asked, "Would anyone at the clown retirement home know why Alvin changed his name? And if there is another clown called Dazzle?"

"They might," Kiki answered. "Would you like the address of the retirement home?"

Chapter 18

Having never been to a clown retirement home before, I didn't know what to expect. But I wasn't expecting a crumbling detached house down a country lane.

As we pulled into the gravelled car park attached to the crumbling building, Peggy said, "It's not much to look at, is it? I was expecting lots of bright colours for some reason. Maybe some flowers in pots, or some funny garden ornaments." She wrinkled her nose. "This looks more like a property waiting for demolition. Have we got the right address?"

I nodded. "Perhaps it's different on the inside."

"Let's hope so. I've got a funny feeling we're going to find out something interesting inside."

"Funny like laughing? Or funny like it's related to Dazzle's death?"

"The latter. I hope. Should we stop calling him Dazzle?"

She nodded. "Good idea. Gloomy suits him better."

"I was thinking we should call him by his real name. Alvin Peel, wasn't it?"

"Okay, let's call him by that. I still prefer Gloomy, though."

We got out of the car and headed towards the drab-looking structure. Bits of plaster were hanging off above the door, and paint was peeling from the window frames.

Peggy looked the building over in pity. "I wonder how the retired clowns survive once they stop performing. Do they have pensions? Or do they survive on pity and donations? Perhaps they have to turn a few tricks now and again to bring in some pennies."

"Turn a few tricks?" I asked with a smile. "What kind of tricks?"

"Get your mind out of the gutter, missy. You know what I meant." She pressed the silver doorbell in front of us.

All of a sudden, a thin jet of water shot out from the middle of the doorbell and hit Peggy in the face.

I was too stunned to do anything. I just gawped at her.

Peggy stared at me open-mouthed as water trickled down her face. Then she burst out laughing.

"Peggy? Are you okay?" I asked, my mouth involuntarily turning up at each corner.

Peggy flapped her hand at the doorbell. "The...bell...water!" Her laughs turned into hoots. She put one hand on her side, and used the other to steady herself on the door.

I took a clean tissue from my handbag and held it out to her. She was too hysterical with laughter to take it, so I wiped the water from her face, and then put the soggy tissue back in my bag.

Peggy finally composed herself, wiped her tears of mirth away, and said, "Why hasn't anyone come to the door? Do we have to press the bell again?"

"I hope not."

Peggy turned her twinkling eyes on me. "You press it."

I took a step back. "I will not."

"Go on."

"Nope." I looked at the door. "But I'll knock on the door. It looks safe enough."

"Famous last words," Peggy said, which didn't reassure me at all.

Gingerly, and like I was touching dynamite, I gently tapped on the door.

Peggy and I braced ourselves for whatever was going to happen next.

Nothing did.

"Now what?" Peggy asked. "Is there even anyone inside?"

I moved towards the letterbox, leaned over, and carefully pushed it open. It creaked slightly. I was about to shout out a hello, when a pair of eyes suddenly popped up right in front of me.

I was too scared to speak. I stared at the eyes. And the eyes stared back at me. Peggy came to my aid and pulled me away from the letterbox, which was a good job because I could have been stuck in that staring position forever.

The door suddenly swung open, and a small clown stood there with open arms and a wide grin on a painted face. For a moment, I thought it was a child, but a glance at the many wrinkles beneath the face paint told me I was looking at an elderly clown. Possibly one of the retired ones?

Before we could say anything, the little clown broke into a happy dance and a jaunty song of welcome. His deep voice quite startled me. He was a blur of red and yellow as he jigged from side to side.

When he'd finished singing and dancing, he stood to one side, and bellowed, "Come in! Come in! Leave your cares behind, and come in!"

"Steady on. We're not deaf," Peggy said. She gave her right ear a deliberate rub.

We entered the retirement home for clowns. The sight of the inside of the building rendered us speechless.

The walls were painted the brightest of colours. Eye-wateringly bright. Every colour you could imagine had been flung on the wall in energetic splatters. It was like children had been given tester paint pots from a DIY shop, and then been allowed to go mad with them.

The carpet covering wasn't any calmer. The floor was covered with carpet squares of vivid hues. I couldn't see that any colour matched another one. Where had they got so many different coloured squares from?

Peggy let out a small groan, and said, "My eyes hurt. I feel like I'm having a technicoloured nightmare."

The little clown at our side twirled around, and declared, "Isn't it marvellous? A creative masterpiece!"

Peggy said, "I wouldn't use those words."

The clown suddenly broke into a cartwheel as he travelled along the hallway a little. He came to a stop the right way up, pointed to part of the wall, and said proudly, "I did that bit."

"Great," I said with a nod. "It's lovely."

"Thank you." He bowed, and then cartwheeled back to us almost knocking Peggy over.

Peggy glowered at the clown, and said, "Could you kindly calm down? Your antics are giving me a headache."

Like a naughty child, the clown's eyes went wide, and his hands came up to cover his mouth. He whispered, "Sorry. Are you ready for the show now? We're all waiting."

"A show?" I asked. "What kind of a show?"

The clown continued to whisper. "The most marvellous show you will ever see. Kiki phoned us to say you were coming to visit us. We're very, very excited. We haven't put on a show for a long time."

Peggy began, "We haven't come here for a show. We—"

I gently interrupted her. "A show sounds wonderful."

The clown beamed at us. "Follow me." He skipped off down the hallway.

Peggy shook her head at me. "What have we let ourselves in for?"

Chapter 19

I was grateful we'd been subjected to the vibrant entrance area before meeting the other clowns because they were even brighter than the painted walls and colourful carpet tiles. The large room we were taken into was abundant with many colours. At first, it looked like swathes of silks had been placed decoratively around the room. But as the material moved, it became clear the room was full of people in clown costumes. They looked like living, breathing rainbows. All of them smiled our way, their make-up making their painted-on smiles even bigger.

Peggy nudged me, and whispered, "Should I take a photo of this for Robbie?"

I whispered back, "Why would you do such a cruel thing?"

"In case he ever gets on my nerves." She pursed her lips as she took in the smiling clowns. "On second thoughts, I won't take a photo. I think the bright colours would break the camera on my phone."

The clown who'd brought us into the room led us over to a sofa and invited us to sit down. Excited giggles erupted from the waiting clowns. For the briefest of seconds, I felt like we'd walked into a trap. Maybe these clowns were behind the death of Alvin Peel, and they knew we were on to them.

Peggy must have been reading my thoughts because she said quietly, "I hope we make it out of here alive. Those smiles they're giving us suddenly look sinister."

The clowns fell silent, bowed their heads, and parted like the Red Sea. An elderly female clown in a stripy purple-and-pink outfit stepped forward with her arms open wide.

She aimed the full beam of her smile on us, and said, "You are warmly welcome to our matinee performance. My name is Gertrude Washington, or Giggles as I'm lovingly known." A devilish glint came into her eyes. "I do hope you're not easily offended."

She didn't wait for our answers. Then she proceeded to tell us one smutty joke after another. I had never heard such filthy humour before, and my cheeks felt like they were going to burst into flames of embarrassment. I looked at Peggy and saw how shocked she was too. As a contrast to my red cheeks, Peggy's face was chalk white.

The rest of the clowns weren't shocked whatsoever. They roared with laughter at every joke, which made Gertrude tell further jokes which became increasingly more obscene.

When Gertrude finished, we were treated to a sketch by a clown called Puddles. His act started by him throwing glitter at Peggy and me. Peggy told him in no uncertain terms to shove his glitter where the sun didn't shine. Puddles wasn't upset by her words, and proceeded to dance around the room with an open umbrella.

A few more clowns appeared and showed us what they could do. A lot of creaking and cracking noises came from their elderly bodies, and some of them forgot what they were doing. I kept a polite smile on my face. Peggy only swore a few times, and all under her breath.

When the show was over, Peggy and I gave the clowns an enthusiastic round of applause. Mine was a bit more enthusiastic than Peggy's. Some of the clowns yawned and left the room.

We took the opportunity to talk to individual clowns about Alvin Peel.

That's when things got interesting.

Chapter 20

I spoke to a clown dressed in a tatty costume, but it was only tatty by design because I could see how professionally it had been made. By Kiki? I didn't know whether it was part of his act or not, but whenever he replied to a question, he produced a little gift from one of his many voluminous pockets. Just little trinkets like a yo-yo, a silver paper clip, a tiny tape measurer, and other things you might find in a Christmas cracker.

His clown name was Knickknack, and he had the sweetest smile.

After some general chitchat, I asked him about Alvin Peel.

Knickknack smiled, and said, "You mean Gloomy. He tried his best, but he wasn't a patch on his old dad. You should have seen Gloomy senior in his heyday. Big sad eyes. A forlorn expression. You could feel the sadness coming from in waves. The audiences loved him."

He handed me a large paperclip. I put it in my pocket with the other gifts he'd given me.

"Tell me more about Alvin," I said. I wondered if I should be giving him gifts in return, but I didn't have much to give him other than tissues and bits of make-up.

Knickknack's smile faded a little at my question. "He didn't have the proper disposition for a clown. We do this job because we love making audiences happy, but all Alvin was bothered about were profits. He'd wear advertising logos on his outfits when he performed. And he'd bring merchandise to his shows and would stand at the exit doors waving them in peoples' faces until they bought something. He wasn't even good at his act. Whereas the audiences felt sympathy for Gloomy senior, they didn't feel anything but disgust when Alvin performed. He just had that way about him."

He gave me a little pack of pens. I took them with a smile and thought there must be something suitable in my bag to give him in return. Maybe I had a pen somewhere, or a pack of stamps.

I said, "I saw him perform recently. But he wasn't called Gloomy. He'd changed his clown name to something else."

There was a sudden hush at that point. I saw Peggy looking my way from across the room. Her eyebrows rose in question.

Knickknack's smile faded completely. His voice held a hint of steel as he said, "He did what?"

"He changed his clown name."

The silence was complete now, apart from the rustling of many silk costumes as the clowns turned to look at me. It was an eerie sight, and it sent chills down my spine.

"What did he change his name to?" Knickknack asked me, his voice devoid of all emotion now.

"Dazzle." I waited for a response from the watching clowns.

I got one.

There were outraged cries. Followed by a stream of curse words. Some clowns pulled pom-poms from their costumes, threw them on the floor, and stamped on them in some sort of clown rage.

Then the clowns turned their backs on me. The ones close to Peggy turned their backs on her.

Knickknack held his hand out to me, and said, "I'd like my gifts back."

I pulled the items from my handbag and returned them. Pushing my luck, I said, "Is it normal for a clown to change their name?"

There was no response.

I carried on, "Was there a clown called Dazzle? Is he still alive? Do you know him? Or her?"

A voice piped up from the back of the room, "Don't tell her anything about the accident!"

"It wasn't an accident!" someone else yelled. "He did it on purpose. We all know he did."

"Quiet!" Knickknack roared, making me jump. He glowered at me, pointed to the exit door, and ordered, "Go. Now. Both of you. And don't come back."

Trying not to be intimidated by the clown, I said, "Can't you tell me more about Dazzle? And the accident?"

"Leave. Now. Before I make you leave."

Peggy rushed over to me, took me by the arm, and muttered, "Let's get out of here before there's another murder."

I was still reluctant to leave, but I was no match for a determined Peggy. She had me out of that building and into my car within a minute.

"Put your foot down, Karis," Peggy cried out.

Angry clown faces pressed against the windows of the dilapidated building like something from a horror movie.

I drove out of the car park like a professional racing driver, or so I thought, flinging gravel into the air as we went.

When we were a safe distance away, I finally let out the breath I was holding. So did Peggy.

She said, "I thought we were goners then. We could have been taken prisoner by those demented clowns. They could have brainwashed us and turned us into clowns like them, and then we would have stayed in that house forever! They would have made us paint the wall!"

"Don't exaggerate. I'm sure they wouldn't have done anything like that."

"Did you see the expressions on their faces?" She took a sharp breath. "Karis, they had murder in their eyes, that's what it was. Murder in their eyes. If they knew about Alvin pinching another clown's name, they could have put a contract out on him. A clown contract to kill him."

I tutted. "A clown contract. That's just silly."

"Is it? We need to find out more about that accident they mentioned."

I nodded. "Yes, and we should find out if Dazzle was a real clown, and where he is now."

"Or she," Peggy added. "Dazzle could be female."

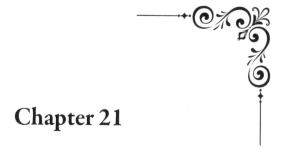

Chapter 21

While I was driving, my phone rang.

"Will you answer that, please?" I asked Peggy. "It might be Erin."

She took my phone from my handbag, looked at the caller display, and said, "It's your boyfriend. Shall I pretend to be you and whisper sweet nothings to him?"

"I've never whispered sweet nothings to anyone. I don't even know what those are."

Peggy took the call. "Hello, DCI Parker. This is Peggy Marshall speaking on behalf of Karis Booth. What is the nature of your call today? Business or pleasure?"

From the corner of my eye, I saw her grinning as she listened to Seb's reply.

She said, "I will relate your request to Ms Booth. Just hold the line a moment. Thank you for your patience." She said to me, "He wants to meet you at home to talk about our murder investigation. Are you available within the next hour?"

"I am. We'll go home now."

Peggy resumed her conversation with Seb. "Ms Booth will be available to meet with you soon. Our estimated time of arrival at Ms Booth's home will be approximately twenty minutes, depending on the traffic situation." She went silent as she listened to Seb's reply. "Yes, I did say *our* murder investigation. Have you got a problem with that?" She went quiet again for a little while before saying, "I don't care for your tone, DCI Parker. If you were doing your job properly then we wouldn't have to make our own investigations, would we? I am ending this call now. Goodbye."

She tutted as she put my phone back in my bag. "That man is so rude. Telling me to keep my nose out of police business. The cheek of him."

I smiled. "I know. The absolute cheek. Did he say what he wanted to talk about?"

"No. But I'm sure you'll find out soon. He seemed eager to talk with you. Karis, do you want me to find out more about that accident? I can go online. I'm quite good at finding things out now. Even things I shouldn't. You have to be careful what you type into the search bar, you know. I've discovered some things I didn't want to."

"I can well imagine," I replied.

"You don't have to imagine it, I'll tell you what I found."

"You don't have to."

"I don't mind. And it'll take my mind off those horrible clowns. I'm starting to feel sympathy for Robbie now."

Peggy began to tell me about her online searches, and what she'd found quite by accident. I almost veered off the road at one point.

It wasn't long before we reached the pair of semi-detached houses where we lived side by side. Peggy had been Mum and Dad's neighbour for years, and I couldn't imagine not having her next door.

Seb was leaning against his car looking very handsome in his dark blue business suit. With a smile on his face, he watched us get out of the car.

Peggy waved at him, and called out, "I can't stay to chat. I'm following up a lead on our murder investigation." She chuckled to herself as she went down the path to her house. I could still hear her laughing as she went inside the house.

Seb shook his head at her. "She'll be the death of me one day." His look was soft as he gazed at me. "I assume you're going to tell me what you and Peggy have been up to."

"I will. But I'd like to know what you've got to say first."

"Okay. I've just had an interesting conversation with Johanna Mullen about a confrontation she had with Alvin Peel at the party. Shall we go inside?"

He sneakily caught hold of my hand as we headed into my house. With his other hand, he cast a cheery wave at Peggy who was peeping out of her window. She winked, before disappearing from view.

I made a cup of tea for Seb and myself, and then we sat at the kitchen table.

He said, "I spoke to Johanna a few hours ago. She had a confrontation with Alvin Peel in the kitchen after his first performance."

"After he'd insulted Dean and Klaudia?"

"Yes. She wasn't happy about what he'd said to them. Understandably. So, she spoke to him, and said he should apologise. And that he should make his apology public."

"What did he say to that?"

Seb gave me a tight smile. "Alvin said he had nothing to apologise for, and that he was merely telling the truth. At which point, he made a pass at Johanna."

"He did? Really?"

He smiled. "Don't look so surprised. She's an attractive woman."

I only bristled a little at that comment. I managed to say, "I suppose she is."

Seb placed his hand over mine. "She's not as beautiful as you."

"Excellent response. How did he make a pass?"

"Do you really need the details?"

"Yes. Was it a comment? Or a physical thing?"

Seb replied, "He made some comments about how beautiful she was, and then asked her out on a date. When she refused, he pulled her close and kissed her."

I nodded. "That would explain why she was wiping her cheek when she came out of the kitchen. I noticed she'd gone in there after Alvin. He must have got face paint on her cheek when he kissed her."

"Nothing gets past you." He took a drink of his tea, leaned back in the chair, and asked, "So, tell me what you and Peggy have been up to. Don't leave anything out."

"In my defence, I was going to leave the investigation to you."

"That's considerate of you," he replied with a twinkle in his eyes.

"But I couldn't leave everything to you because Jen at the café thought I might fall down the steps and hurt myself."

Seb sat up straighter. "What do you mean? Did you nearly fall down the steps? Is there something wrong with them? Do you want me to take a look at them?"

"No, nothing like that." I explained about the problematic third step from the top. Then I told him about following Dean, our visit to Klaudia's house, our return journey to Kiki's home, and our meeting with the clowns.

By the time I'd finished, Seb needed another cup of tea. I refused another as I was still drinking the first one.

When Seb had made himself another cup of tea, he sat down and looked at me for a few moments.

I said, "You look as if you're deciding whether to tell me something or not."

"I am. I'll tell you anyway. You know about the back door being broken in the kitchen."

"I do."

"We've checked the CCTV footage. Or tried to. The cameras had been damaged. Someone had sprayed paint over the nearest two cameras which cover the rear area of the café."

I frowned. "Wouldn't the cameras show that happening? If someone came up and aimed paint at them?"

Seb nodded. "There are images of someone doing that. It was a clown."

"No!"

"Yes. And it looked like Dazzle."

"No!" I exclaimed again. "The dead Dazzle? Alvin Peel? Or someone who had the same face paint as him?"

"It's hard to tell. His face was only visible for a few seconds. But here's the strange thing. The cameras were damaged about an hour before the party began."

It took me a few moments to realise what that meant. "So, does that mean Alvin vandalised the cameras because he was planning to do something which he didn't want anyone to see?"

Seb nodded, and prompted me, "Or?"

"Or it wasn't Alvin who vandalised the cameras? It was someone who looked like him, maybe the elusive real Dazzle. And the real Dazzle did that because he was planning to kill Alvin?" I rubbed my head. "I'm confusing myself."

"I think you could be on to something, though. Now that we know Alvin possibly stole the identity of another clown, we've got another suspect to take into account."

I slowly nodded. "Someone who had a grudge against Alvin. But who?"

"The original Dazzle?" Seb suggested.

I said, "Or someone who knew the original Dazzle? We could be looking at a woman who was related to, or who knew the original Dazzle."

"You think a woman could have done this?"

"You never know. Once a person is covered in that much face paint, it's hard to tell if they're male or female."

Seb's phone beeped. He checked it, sighed, and said, "I have to go back to the station. Let's catch up later. Do you think you can leave the investigation to me now? And I ask that with a lot of respect for your psychic powers."

"I'll try. But I can't promise anything."

I walked him to the front door.

Before he walked away, he said, "If possible, keep away from those steps at the café. Please."

"I will."

As soon as he'd driven off, Peggy came rushing out of her house. She held a piece of paper aloft. "Karis! I've found out what the accident was! Well, I think I have. Get your car keys. We have to go to the pub."

"This is hardly the time for a gin and tonic."

"It's always time for a gin and tonic, but that's not why I want to visit the pub. It's one pub in particular. It used to be a theatre."

"Oh?" She had my interest now.

She smiled triumphantly. "The theatre was closed down following an accident. There's not much information online, but there is one interesting part online." She paused for dramatic effect. "The accident involved a clown."

Chapter 22

As we drove along, I told Peggy about the CCTV cameras being vandalised by a person who looked like Dazzle.

"Interesting," she said with a nod. "So, the murder was planned. Very interesting."

We arrived at the pub which was located off the main street of a nearby town. The old theatre had been taken over by one of those big-name companies who renovate old buildings and make them useful again. Useful if you like going to the pub, that is. Which Peggy did because she rubbed her hands together gleefully as we walked towards the unimaginatively named "The Old Theatre."

Inside, a lot of the existing features had been kept. Even the original stage was there, albeit with tables and chairs on it now. Balconies ran along either side of the stage, and contained people who were consuming food and drink. The main area of the pub, which I assumed was where the stalls had once been, contained more tables and chairs. The chairs had been upholstered in red velvet that matched the heavy-looking curtains on either side of the stage which were pinned back.

The bar was at the rear of the large room, and a handful of people were waiting to be served.

Peggy rubbed her hands together again, and declared, "The drinks are on me. Karis, what do you want? A stiff drink after facing those terrifying clowns. I'm going to get myself a small gin and tonic."

Without waiting for my answer, she moved swiftly over to the bar and shoved her way in between a couple of burly men.

I followed her, and said, "I'll have a soft drink, please. An orange juice will be fine, thanks."

One of the burly men started to give their order to the young woman behind the counter, but a firm cough from Peggy made him say, "Oh, sorry. You go first."

"Thank you, young man," Peggy replied with a demure look which I didn't know she was capable of making. She addressed the woman with a firm, "A small gin and tonic, and an orange juice. Thank you."

Once we had our drinks, we began to wander around the pub. I had noticed stairs leading to the balconies when we first came in. I wondered if they had anything to do with my vision of someone falling. Were these the stairs from my vision? I pointed them out to Peggy, and we headed to the stairs on the left.

When we got there, I stared at the carpeted steps and waited for a vision to come to me. Nothing happened.

"Walk up them," Peggy suggested. She took a big slug of her drink, and smacked her lips together in appreciation. "Be careful on the third step from the top, just in case. Don't worry, I'll catch you if you fall." She took another drink which made me wonder if she'd be the one who would end up falling down.

I carefully went up the steps, half expecting a vision to appear. I paused when a distant sound came to me for a second. It was so brief that I almost missed it. It was the noise of an audience laughing. The same sound I'd heard in the café near the steps just before the shadowy figure had fallen.

Despite going slowly up and down the stairs three times, I didn't get any funny feelings apart from an ache in my knees. But there was nothing paranormal about that, just age.

Peggy had almost finished her drink by the time I'd done cavorting up and down the steps like some sort of fitness freak who couldn't afford to go to the gym.

I said, "Nothing happening here. Let's go to the right-hand side. I'll try those."

She nodded, downed her drink in one go, and announced, "I'll get a refill as we pass the bar."

I waited while Peggy got her drink, and then we went to the other stairs. Again, I performed the peculiar routine of ascending and descending the carpet-covered steps. All the while, Peggy stood at the bottom and cried out, "Anything yet? Any tingles? Weird smells? Strange sounds?"

Anyone watching us would have thought we weren't right in the head, but that didn't stop us. That brief sound of an audience kept floating back to me, but only for a second or two each time.

By the time I descended for the fourth time, I saw a stern-looking security guard standing next to Peggy. He was glowering at Peggy, and she was staring intently at the carpet as if wishing she could make herself invisible.

As I got closer, the man said, "I think it's time I had a chat with you two ladies. I'd like to know why you're acting so suspiciously."

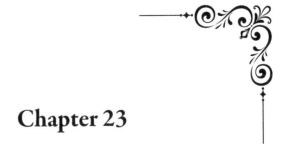

Chapter 23

Peggy appeared to be looking for an escape route. I didn't want her leaving me alone to face the security guard, so I discreetly moved to her side so that she couldn't run away.

The man raised one eyebrow at us. His stern look intensified. "Well? What have you got to say for yourselves?"

"Nothing!" Peggy declared loudly. "We've done nothing wrong. We are innocent women. And you can't prove otherwise. You will not sully our reputations with your wild accusations!"

"Madam, I haven't accused you—"

Peggy cut him off. "You have accusation written all over your face. It's even in those eyebrows of yours. You won't take us down easily. We'll put up a good fight." She drained her glass, slammed it down on a nearby table, and then jabbed her fists in the air at the guard.

Just how many drinks had she consumed? Had she been sneaking off to the bar every time I'd had my back to her?

I gently brought her jabbing fists to her sides, and said to her, "Give him the chance to speak."

The security guard adjusted his tie as if doing so would give him more authority under Peggy's hard stare. He said, "I saw you two acting suspiciously. I'm always on the lookout for behaviour of a dubious nature. It's part of my job." His chin lifted as he got into his flow. "And when I see people of a shifty nature, I have to check it out, and make sure they're not up to no good. It's my job, you see."

Peggy's eyes narrowed. "Are you calling us shifty now? That's hardly polite, is it? Or is having bad manners part of your job too? Or is that just your nature? Were you born that way?"

He adjusted his tie again as he carefully searched for his next words.

I felt a rush of sympathy for the man. I wasn't about to reveal the real reason as to why we were there, so I thought of a watered-down version which I hoped he'd believe.

With a look at the steps in front of me, I said, "This might seem crazy, but I heard a story about an accident occurring here years ago. It involved a set of steps. We're interested in accidents like that." I suddenly became aware of how ghoulish I sounded. I tried to make the best out of the hole I was digging for myself. "We're interested in local history, even if it's sometimes gruesome."

The guard didn't look convinced.

Undeterred, I continued, "We heard that a performer fell from somewhere near the top of the stairs."

"Perhaps the third step from the top," Peggy said matter-of-factly. She shrugged. "Maybe the fourth or fifth. We're not sure."

A spark of interest alighted in the guard's eyes. Lowering his voice a little, he asked, "Does this accident involve a clown by any chance?"

Peggy and I nodded enthusiastically.

The guard looked left and right, moved a little closer, and said, "Do you want to see something amazing? Something not many people have seen in a long time?"

Peggy backed up a bit. "I hope you're not talking about anything smutty, young man." She pointed to his name badge. "Are you even a real security guard, Eric? Or have you dressed up so you can lure women away to see something amazing that isn't that amazing at all? Hmm?"

Colour rushed to Eric's cheeks. "What? No. No! I didn't mean anything like that. And I am a genuine security guard. I've got a certificate to prove it."

Peggy looked as if she were going to ask him to produce his security certificate. Before she could, I said, "What would you like to show us? Is it related to the accident which happened to the clown?"

Keeping a wary eye on Peggy, he replied, "Yes, it does have something to do with that clown. I can't recall his name just at the moment, but I know he was famous around here. There are rumours he'd been spotted by a talent agent and was going to America. But then the accident happened, and he never worked again. Or so I heard."

I nodded. "So, he survived the accident."

Eric scratched his head. "I think so. Anyway, some of the original stage equipment is still here along with some old stage props. I don't know if they're going to use them for anything, or if they're just storing them for some reason. But the equipment's still here. It's in the cellar."

My excitement rose. "Can we have a look in the cellar?"

"Please?" Peggy asked in a suddenly friendly voice. "Eric, you look like an accommodating kind of man who would go out of his way to help a person. Like a modern-day hero." She gave him a big smile.

The man's chest puffed out proudly. "I like to do my best. I'll just make sure it's okay with management. The public aren't normally allowed down there. Although, we do have ghost tours in this building from time to time, and the public are allowed in the cellar then."

"Ghost tours?" I asked. "Is this building haunted?"

"Some say it is," he replied. "But I've never seen anything. Maybe you need that sixth-sense thing to see ghosts. Or some sort of psychic ability. That kind of nonsense. Wait here while I have an official word with the bosses."

He walked away with a spring in his step, obviously happy to be helping members of the public who had a penchant for the macabre.

I suddenly shivered.

Peggy noticed, and asked, "What's going on? Are you having a vision?"

"No, but I'm about to."

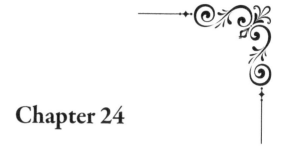

Chapter 24

I didn't have a vision, not straight away. It came to me a little later.

As we waited for the return of the security guard, I saw Peggy casting a longing look at her empty glass.

"Don't even think about it," I said. "I need you to have a clear head."

"Spoilsport," she muttered. Then she broke into a grin. "You're probably right. I think those gins were making me aggressive. I was ready to box Eric's ears when I first saw him. I don't want to get a reputation for being a fighter. Not at my age." She tipped her head. "Although, a reputation of any sort at my age would be something."

Eric came back with a smug smile on his face. He said, "The bosses weren't too happy to let you go to the cellar, but I used my powers of persuasion, and they soon changed their minds. But if you injure yourselves in any way, the management reserve the right to refuse any claims of compensation. Management want to make it clear you're entering the cellar at your own risk."

"Fair enough," Peggy said. "Let's get going, then. We haven't got all day."

"Follow me," Eric ordered, suddenly full of himself. "And stay behind me. You don't have the authority to open the door to the cellar."

Peggy rolled her eyes at me before following Eric.

I thought the building was probably one hundred years old, possibly even older. So, I was expecting the cellar to be dark, dusty and damp. But I was wrong. As we went down the stone steps, we were greeted by a large and airy room which had a high ceiling. The white

83

brick walls looked freshly painted, and the floor was paved with clean, stone slabs. Large archways separated the cellar into sections. The area in front of us contained barrels of beer and lager, and bottles of many varieties of wine lined the shelves.

Peggy muttered, "Not a bad place to be locked in for the night."

The guard led us through the two arches until we came to the back of the cellar. Here, we found a huge selection of stage props. Everything from fading costumes on rails to threadbare wigs hanging from nails on the wall. Half-open chests showed torn hats, broken shoes and tatty feather boas. I felt like each item could tell us a tale or two. Not that I was going to start talking to inanimate objects.

Despite the faded glory of the items, there was almost a regal feel about them. As if we were standing in the middle of an important part of history.

My attention went to more props resting against the wall. Pieces of rolled-up backdrops leaned drunkenly against the wall. Faded street signs were barely readable. Closed boxes kept the mystery of whatever was inside them.

And then I saw them.

The steps from my vision. Or almost. These stairs were open with no backs to them, but despite that, I knew for certain I was looking at the right ones.

They were leaning against the wall.

Steps going nowhere.

I was aware of Peggy chatting to Eric about being a wine connoisseur, and would he like her to sample any of the pub's drinks. He said no, so Peggy tried a different approach, but I didn't listen because I felt a vision coming to me.

Peggy and Eric's voices faded as I stared at the wooden steps. I couldn't take my eyes off them. Like a magnet pulling me, I felt myself being drawn forward.

Before I knew what I was doing, I was walking up the steps.

When I got to the small platform at the top, I slowly turned around and looked out.

That was when a vivid vision came to me.

Chapter 25

The low rumble of applause came to me from an invisible audience. The noise escalated, and the cellar faded from view to be replaced with the inside of the theatre in its heyday. I was on the stage looking out at ghostly faces from the past who were clapping enthusiastically in my direction. A faint fragrance came to me from the audience, a mixture of perfume and cigarette smoke.

I felt a tingling all over my body, and when I looked down at myself, I could see the shimmer of a glittery costume covering my body. Red sequins caught in the light of an unseen floodlight. Was I taking on Dazzle's presence? Was that even possible if he was still alive? Or had he passed away recently and I was being possessed by a dead clown?

Neither option bothered me. Suddenly, all I cared about was the adoration coming from the audience. I felt like I was the king of all clowns. I could do anything. Say anything. And I would have this audience eating out of my hands. Nothing could go wrong for me. I was on top of the world.

With a theatrical flourish of my hand, I took a bow. The applause became deafening. I heard excited chants of, "Dazzle! Dazzle!" My mouth widened in a paint-covered smile. I could feel the power running through me. Every day of hard work over the years was finally paying off. Not only did I have this town in love with me, I would soon be leaving for America. Oh, they would love me over there too. They would adore me.

Comical music sounded out. Time for the show to begin.

I took a step down performing my perfected jiggle. The jiggle which made me look as if the steps were too slippery, and I was going to fall at any second. But it was all part of my act.

Another step. More jiggling. Some of the audience gasped as if expecting me to fall. They must be new to my show. The rest of the crowd gave me knowing smiles.

I placed my foot on the third step from the top. Before I could perform my professional jiggle, something unexpected happened.

A hand shot through the gap in the stairs. It roughly grabbed my ankle and yanked it backwards, sending pain shooting up my leg. I felt myself falling forward.

The world turned upside down as I tumbled down the steps. The audience clapped louder.

Time slowed down. The ground came slowly closer. A strange cushiony feeling surrounded me.

I landed at the bottom of the steps and was aware of excruciating pain shooting through my body. But it wasn't real pain, more like the thought of pain.

The applause abruptly stopped, and the screaming started.

Ghostly thoughts of pain returned to me. It seemed the worst of it was in my back. From my prone position on the ground, I tried to move, but my limbs wouldn't budge. I managed to turn my head so that I could look towards the steps. I caught a glimpse of a painted face watching me from behind the steps. Despite the downward painted smile, he was grinning broadly.

Was it...?

Before I could focus on the face, I was brought out of my vision by the scream of someone I knew.

It was Peggy. She was on her knees at my side, and yelling my name right in my ear.

"Don't move!" she cried out.

"I can't move," I replied. "Peggy, stop shouting."

"I can't help it!" Her voice was hysterical now.

Eric said, "Move to one side. I know first aid. Let me check the victim."

"Don't call her a victim! She's still alive."

I wasn't sure how alive I was, or what was broken. I couldn't feel any pain, but was that a good thing or a bad thing?

I let the security guard check me over. Tingles went through me, and I gingerly wiggled my fingers and toes. Then I moved my arms, despite Peggy screaming at me and telling me not to move.

All of a sudden, a certainty came to me. A certainty that I wasn't injured. I recalled the cushiony feeling which had surrounded me as I fell. Had ghostly hands assisted me?

Slowly and carefully, I got to my feet. Peggy shouted at me again, and told me to keep still, but I told her I didn't feel in pain at all. I carefully stretched my arms and legs. They felt fine. I leaned to either side. Again, everything felt okay. I even did a little jog on the spot, which is not something I normally do.

Peggy raised her hands to the ceiling, and declared loudly, "It's a miracle! A real miracle!"

Eric muttered something about us needing to sign a waiver before hurrying away.

Peggy gave me a very gentle hug. When she released me, she stared into my eyes, and asked, "Are you okay? Really okay?"

I nodded. "I feel fine."

"What happened? What did you see?"

"I saw Dazzle falling. Someone grabbed his ankle. And I think I know who it was."

Chapter 26

Before I could go into detail, Peggy said firmly, "I'm taking you to the hospital. I want you checked over from top to toe."

"But I feel fine." I performed a little dance to confirm my words.

"I don't care how you feel. You could be in shock, and some chemicals zipping around your body could be making you think you're okay. You could collapse at any moment. Come on. This isn't a discussion."

She had that look on her face which meant any protesting from me was futile.

I tried anyway. "Honestly, I do feel fine."

In reply, Peggy gently took my elbow as if I were a feather which would blow away, and carefully led me across the cellar. We made slow progress up the stone stairs and through the pub. Peggy kept yelling at people to get out of the way. Which they did.

The security guard was suspiciously absent.

When we got to the car park, Peggy said, "Give me your car keys."

I stiffened. "What for?"

"Because I'm going to drive. What else would I need them for? Hand them over."

"But you haven't driven in years. Not after that incident with the bus."

"Pah!" she said with a wave of her hands. "That's ancient history. Anyway, driving a car is like riding a bike. You just get back in the saddle and everything comes flooding back." She wiggled her fingers at me. "Keys. I'm not going to let you drive. You're still in shock. Didn't you say your car was insured for all drivers over a certain age, and with driving experience?"

"I did." Knowing I was beaten, I reluctantly gave her the keys. But I tried once more to stop her. "We can get the bus, you know. And you have had a couple of drinks."

"Nonsense. Why would we get the bus when we've got a car here? And you falling down those steps sobered me up in an instant. I'm not over the limit anyway." She waved the keys wildly in the air. "Why won't the car open? What's wrong with these keys?"

"Press the little red button."

She did so. The car beeped. Peggy grinned, and said, "It's like magic. Get in. Let's get going." She got in the car and spent a minute adjusting the driver's seat.

If I wasn't in shock before I got in the car, I certainly was afterwards. Peggy was a nightmare driver. She didn't indicate. She thought the red traffic lights were just a suggestion. And if anyone cut her up, she made the most obscene gestures at them. And the speed she went at almost made my hair turn white.

By the time we'd reached the hospital, my palms were sweaty and I had trouble getting out of the car because my legs were trembling so much.

When Peggy saw me, she gave me a satisfied nod. "See, you are in shock. I was right. Once we get inside, leave everything to me. I'll get someone to see you as soon as possible. Do you want a wheelchair? You look like you're going to collapse."

"I'll be fine in a few minutes. I don't need a wheelchair. I don't even need to be looked over."

Her answer was to carefully steer me towards the entrance doors.

I don't know what magic Peggy worked on the staff, but I was checked over by a doctor within thirty minutes. He pronounced me fit and well. Peggy didn't believe him, so he checked again. His diagnosis was just the same.

When Peggy was satisfied, she took me to the hospital café and sat me at a table facing the door. When I asked her why we weren't going straight home, she just gave me a mysterious smile and told me to be patient.

I remained patient while she got us a cup of tea and a slice of cake. She was up to something. I could tell by the evasive look on her face.

As she tucked into her cake, I asked, "Don't you want to know what I saw in my vision? I thought you'd be bursting to know."

"I was more concerned about your health. But now that I know you're okay, you can tell me about your vision."

I proceeded to tell her everything. I concluded with, "I think the clown who grabbed Dazzle's ankle was Gloomy. Going by his dismal looking make-up anyway. We need to get some photos of Gloomy and Dazzle just to make sure. There must be something online. And what about the shows which took place at the theatre? I know it was a while ago but won't there be brochures or something? We need to do some digging."

Peggy gave me an enigmatic smile. "Yes. I agree." She glanced towards the door.

I looked over my shoulder and asked, "Are you expecting someone?"

"Perhaps. Have your cake. Sugar is good for shock." She cast another look at the door.

I never say no to cake, so I got stuck in. Peggy was suspiciously quiet, and every time I asked if something was wrong, she gave me that secretive smile again and said no.

She looked towards the door for the tenth time, jumped to her feet, and said, "About bloomin' time."

I turned in my seat to see Seb walking swiftly towards us. There was a worried look on his face. I immediately wondered who'd died.

Before I could get the chance to ask him that, he pulled me to my feet and into his arms. He squeezed me tightly. With a voice thick with emotion, he said, "Peggy told me you nearly died."

My reply was muffled, seeing as I was so squashed against his chest. "I didn't die. I fell down some steps. I've been checked over twice by a doctor. I'm in good health. Nothing broken."

"This time," Peggy added unhelpfully. "Anyway, I'll leave you two lovebirds to it. I've got things to do. I'll get the bus. Bye for now."

I tried to ask her where she was going, but she scuttled out of the café like a woman on a mission. Which, I suspected, she was.

It was another twenty seconds before Seb released me. Which I didn't mind because he was nice to hug.

He said, "I got a lift here because Peggy said you weren't in a fit position to drive. I can I drive you home now."

"You don't have to. I can drive myself."

He put his hands on my shoulders. "Karis, just let me do something for you. Okay? If you're not in shock, then I certainly am. I thought you were at death's door going by Peggy's text."

"When did she even text you? The sneaky thing. And where is she going now? She's up to something. Shall we follow her? You must be good at following people."

"We're not going to follow her. I'm taking you home. You can tell me on the way what happened to put you in such danger."

Once we were in the car, I told Seb about our visit to the pub, and what I'd seen in my vision. He didn't answer as he was concentrating on driving. He was a much better driver than Peggy even though he did go over the speed limit a little.

By the time we came to a stop outside my house, a muscle was twitching in Seb's cheek.

"Are you angry?" I asked him.

"Yes, but not with you. I'm going to get this investigation settled quickly. I don't want you having any more dangerous visions. I'll interview everyone again. If there's a connection to the original Dazzle from someone who was at the party, I'll find it." His look turned softer. "And I would very much appreciate it if you could leave everything to me."

"I'm not sure I can," I answered truthfully. "I can't help getting visions. You know that."

"I do, but try to—" He sighed, shook his head, and continued, "Be careful. That's all. Be careful."

"I will. How are you getting on with the case? If you're allowed to tell me, that is."

"I can tell you. I was going to ask for your help on something anyway. We've got video footage from the party. From mobile phones. You know what people are like for recording everything these days."

"Do you want me to look at the videos and see if I pick up on anything?"

"That's exactly what I'd like you to do. And you can do it from the safety of your home. I'll send the videos via email. Is that okay?"

"It is. Have you got time for a cuppa?"

"No, thanks. I'm getting straight back to the investigation. I'll phone someone to take me to the station."

I offered, "I can do that."

His look gave me his answer. I felt like an invalid again as he took me into my house. He settled me on the sofa and made me a cup of tea. A quick kiss and he was gone.

But I wasn't on my own for long.

Peggy turned up about twenty minutes later with a flushed face and glitter in her hair.

She plopped herself on the sofa next to me, and said, "You'll never guess where I've been."

Chapter 27

I gave the glitter in Peggy's hair a pointed look, and said, "Have you been back to the clowns' retirement home by any chance?"

She looked disappointed. "Yes. How did you know? Did you use your psychic powers?"

"No, There's glitter in your hair. And you look angry as if you've been shouting at someone."

"I've been shouting at many people. They tried to shout back, but I was having none of it." She nodded as if recalling her conversation. "They even tried to throw me out, but I wouldn't go. That fella who threw glitter at us earlier had a go at me too. Threw two handfuls of the stuff at me! As if that was going to stop me. Well, I showed them. I told them I wouldn't leave until I got some information from them."

"And did you?"

"I did. I was so mad at what had happened to you in the pub cellar, that I barged into that house without even knocking. I found those clowns all grouped together laughing as if everything was all right in the world."

I could see she was going to launch into a full description of what had happened, but I cut her short. "What did you find out?"

"I was just getting to that. It seems Dazzle and Gloomy were good friends at one point. Hang on, I won't call him Gloomy when we know full well we're talking about Alvin Peel."

"That's a good point. Keep things simple."

"I'll try. Dazzle and Alvin worked a lot of shows together. But Alvin became increasingly jealous about how positively the audience responded to Dazzle's performances. He thought he should get the same recognition, but we already know Alvin wasn't good with a crowd. He often got drunk and complained to anyone who would listen that Dazzle didn't deserve the success he was getting. He got quite nasty by all accounts. It wasn't long before Alvin began to make veiled threats. And not long after, Dazzle started to have a run of bad luck during his performances."

"Such as?"

"The wrong props being put out." She waved her hand dismissively. "I can't remember the details. But the incidents continued, until the last one with Dazzle falling down the steps. He claims he saw Alvin's face between the gaps of the steps, and that it was him who grabbed his ankle causing him to fall. Just like in your vision. But when Alvin was confronted, he said he had an alibi for the time of the accident."

I frowned. "Did he?"

Peggy pulled a look of disgust. "He said he was with a woman who worked at the theatre. She confirmed it."

"Really?"

Peggy's disgust grew. "Apparently, he was a bit of a ladies man. He had many women on the go at the same time. He could have got his lady friend to lie for him. That's what I think anyway."

I thought back to the vision I'd had. "Maybe I was wrong about the face behind the steps. But that's the name which I heard in my head as I came out of the vision, as if I were still having Dazzle's thoughts. Maybe I've got the wrong clown."

"I don't think you did. According to that bunch of clowns, even though Alvin had an alibi, no one believed him. But no one could prove it. Hang on a minute, this might help." She scrambled about in her handbag and brought out her phone. She tapped on the screen, and then held the phone up to me. "I found some photos on the wall at the retirement home. Is this the face you saw?"

A clown's face was on the screen. His make-up was black and white, the only colour being his slightly bloodshot eyes.

I'd seen that face before.

"That's him!" I declared. "He was smiling when I saw him, but it's definitely the same clown. Is it Alvin?"

"It is."

"I confirmed with the clowns it was Alvin Peel." She moved on to a different photo, and showed it to me. "Do you know who this is?"

My blood ran cold. "It's Dazzle. The original one. Am I right?"

"You are."

"But who is he? What's his real name?"

Peggy lowered her phone. "The clowns don't know. Or if they do know, they wouldn't tell me, no matter how forcibly I asked them."

I sighed. "That doesn't help us at all."

"It doesn't get any better. Dazzle stopped working as a clown after his accident. His injuries were too severe for him to continue. He left the theatre without saying goodbye to anyone. And no one knows what happened to him, or where he went."

We looked at each other for a moment, at a loss for words.

I said, "But he must be around somewhere. He must have found out Alvin was using his name, and then he got his revenge. Maybe."

Peggy nodded. "Yes. But what if Dazzle died years ago, and some relative of his saw what Alvin had done and they decided to take revenge on Dazzle's behalf?"

"A relative? Like a daughter or son? Maybe a wife?"

"Yes." She pressed her lips together as she gathered her thoughts. "Or we could be going down the wrong path altogether. Maybe it was Dean who killed Alvin because of the things Alvin said to him at the party."

"I don't think so. I got the vision of Dazzle falling down the steps for a reason. A reason which is connected to Alvin's death. All we have to do is find out who the real Dazzle was."

"The man who vanished from the face of the earth? The man who could be dead or alive?"

I gave her a cheerful smile. "That's the one."

Chapter 28

Peggy said, "I'm going to nip home to get this disgusting glitter out of my hair."

"You can do that here."

"No, I don't want it all over your carpet. I won't be long."

Once she'd gone, I decided to look at the videos which Seb had sent to me. I sighed when I saw how many there were. But it had to be done. There could be something important on them.

I soon became engrossed in the videos. I didn't know how Seb had convinced people to hand their phones over as some of the videos were quite personal and contained private conversations. But he did have the law on his side. I felt a bit weird watching them, as if I were spying on them. But I soon got over that feeling.

Peggy returned a short while later and joined me at the kitchen table. She said, "What are you looking at now? Something online?"

I explained where the videos had come from, and that Seb was hoping I'd pick up on something.

She moved her chair a bit closer. "Let's have a good look at them. I'm not sure I like watching private videos, but I'll give it a go for the sake of our investigation. Karis, look at that!"

"What?"

"That." She pointed to a corner of the screen. Can you zoom in?"

I did so.

"Ooo," we both said at the same time.

The image showed Klaudia and the mystery dark-haired man standing in a corner of the cafe. The man blatantly had his hand on Klaudia's rounded tummy. Their heads were very close together as they smiled at each other.

Peggy said, "He must be the father of her child. Why else would he be looking at her like that?"

I nodded in agreement. "But look at Alvin's face. He's standing just behind them, and looking very smug."

"He must have worked out what was going on between them. Maybe he tried to blackmail Klaudia or the mystery man. He seemed the type. Let's see if we can find any more videos with our mystery man in them."

We went through more footage from different phones, and it wasn't long before we did find the dark-haired man. He spent more time with Klaudia before moving around the room talking to other people and their children. He walked over to Primrose and chatted with her for a few minutes. Even though the video we were watching was a bit choppy, it was easy to see the love he had in his eyes for the little girl.

Peggy must have noticed it too because she said quietly, "That's fatherly love. I saw it often in your dad's eyes when he looked at you and Erin."

The mention of my dad brought sudden tears to my eyes. It didn't matter how many years had passed since he'd died, the grief was always ready to return at a moment's notice. I quickly blinked my tears away.

Peggy gave my arm a gentle squeeze before saying, "Let's see where our mystery man goes next."

We sat up a bit straighter in our seats when we saw the man talking to Alvin. The dark-haired man had his back to us, so we couldn't see his expression. But we saw how Alvin smirked at whatever the man was saying.

"I wonder if they're talking about Klaudia," Peggy said. "There's a lot of background noise on this video. Can you do something about that? Can you cut that noise out and zoom in on Alvin's conversation? I've seen people do that on crime shows on the TV."

"Would that be people from the FBI or some such organisation?" I asked her. "I don't know how to cut the background noise out. I don't even know if my phone will do that. But I can turn the volume up. That might help."

"It'll have to do. But if we're going to become professional detectives, we should learn some technical skills. I wonder of they do courses at the library. I'll ask them next time I pop in."

I looked at her. "We're not becoming professional detectives."

She raised one eyebrow. "And yet, here we are again, having to do Seb's job for him. I don't know how he'd manage without us."

I shook my head at her words, and then turned my attention back to the video. I started it from the beginning again to enable us to hear Alvin's conversation with the mystery man in full. But when I turned the volume up, the background noise became almost deafening.

Peggy leaned closer to the screen and peered at the two men as if trying to read their lips.

I tried to focus on them too, but some words coming from a different direction caught my attention. My glance went to the person at the bottom of the screen whose words seemed suddenly louder than anything else coming from the video.

It was the birthday girl, Primrose. She was talking on a phone to someone. Was it her mum's phone? Or her dad's? Even though she was only six, it didn't surprise me that she was using a phone. She was probably more articulate with a smartphone than I was.

As she spoke, a strange sensation came over me. It was like when someone finally gives you an answer to a puzzle which has been bamboozling you for days. Or when you couldn't think of an actor's name, and then it suddenly comes to you out of the blue.

I paused the video, looked at Peggy, and said, "There's someone who isn't on our list of suspects."

Peggy looked at the paused video. "You don't mean little Primrose, do you? Karis, that's taking things too far."

"No, I don't mean her." I paused. "It's the person she's talking to on the phone."

Chapter 29

"Primrose's granddad," Peggy said for the tenth time. "Of course. He would be the right age to be Dazzle. And we don't know anything about him. Only that he was absent from the party."

"That we know of," I pointed out. "Do you remember what Johanna said about why he wasn't there?"

"No. I was too busy sizing her up. I didn't like how she kept looking at Seb. What did she say?"

"He said he was too ill to attend. But what if that was just an excuse, and he really was there? Listen to what Primrose is saying to him."

I played the video again. Peggy winced, and said, "I can't make it out above the rest of the chatter."

"She's asking how he is, and then saying she's having a lovely time. Obviously, I can't hear his side of the conversation, but it appears he's asking lots of questions about Alvin. Primrose tells her granddad exactly what Alvin is wearing, and the tricks he performed. And at one point, she took a photo of Alvin and sent it to her granddad."

"He could just be showing an interest," Peggy suggested.

"I think it's more than an interest. Primrose also tells him Alvin spoke to her dad, and her dad had his angry face on afterwards. And she said Alvin fell down the steps but didn't get hurt because he's a magic clown."

Peggy frowned. "Did she see him falling? I didn't think any of the children had seen that. Poor girl."

"She doesn't seem upset by it. And her granddad must have asked her to repeat the falling down the steps bit because she says it again. He's either deaf or extremely interested in that part of Alvin's act."

"Hmm. I suppose it does make sense if her granddad was Dazzle. But if he's ill at home, how would he get to the café that quickly?"

I gave her a knowing look. "That's the beauty of mobile phones. You could be anywhere when you talk on them, and you can easily lie and say you're somewhere else."

Peggy tutted. "There are times when I think technology has an evil side."

"It's not technology which is evil, it's the people who use it." I started placing the facts together. "If Primrose's granddad was the original Dazzle, and if Alvin was behind the accident which ended his career, then isn't that a good motive for murder?"

Peggy nodded. "I would say so. Especially as Alvin stole Dazzle's identity and then had the audacity to perform at Primrose's party. But it still concerns me how quickly he got to the café to kill Alvin."

Something Seb said previously came to me. "I think he was already at the café. At the kitchen door waiting for the right opportunity. Don't forget that the CCTV cameras had been damaged one hour before the party started."

"Oh, yes. And hadn't the person who'd vandalised them been wearing clown make-up?"

"They were. It was Dazzle's make-up."

We looked at each other for a few moments.

Then Peggy said, "Are you thinking what I'm thinking?"

"That we should phone Seb and let him know about this?"

"I wasn't thinking that at all. I think we should confront Primrose's granddad and see what his reaction is. Can you remember his name?"

"Jerry. I remember Johanna saying that Jerry and Johanna sounded like a double act."

Peggy's eyes grew wide. "Perhaps they are a double act. A murdering double act. Let's go and get them."

I shook my head. "We should let Seb know."

Peggy held her hands out, and said, "But what if we're wrong? What if you tell Seb our suspicions, and he goes round to Jerry and accuses him, and Jerry truly is a poorly man who hasn't left his bed for days? Seb would feel such a buffoon. And you would feel awful for leading him down the garden path. It would put a strain on your relationship, and you'd most likely split up. Would you like that to happen, Karis? Would you? Really?"

I gave her a narrow-eyed look. "Don't use reverse psychology on me."

"I wasn't."

"I can see the twinkle in your eyes. You just want to talk to Jerry and see what he's got to say."

She folded her arms in defence. "I do. I admit it. But I do have a point about us possibly going down the garden path. You've got to agree with me on that."

"I suppose so." I looked back at the screen and focused on the image of little Primrose. "We could just have a word with Jerry. Talk about the party, and then mention Alvin. See how he reacts to that."

I felt a tap on my shoulder. Peggy was standing there with my coat in one hand and my car keys in the other. She said, "No time like the present. Let's go. Are you okay to drive now? Or shall I?"

I stood up. "I'll drive."

Chapter 30

We got in my car, but I didn't switch the engine on. I said to Peggy, "We can't go."

"Why not?"

"Because we don't know where Jerry lives."

"I do." She rattled an address off.

I stared at her a moment before saying, "How do you know that?"

She looked away from me. "I thought it wise to find out that information."

"Why?"

"Just in case we needed to speak to Johanna. In private. At her home. Are you going to start the car now?"

I asked, "Why did you think that?"

She looked at me. "Because I don't trust her. As soon as I saw her, I knew there was something devious about her, like she's keeping a big secret. And I'm not just saying that because of the way she was drooling over your boyfriend. There's something about her that I don't trust."

"You say that about a lot of people."

"And I'm always right." She adjusted her tartan coat over her knees. "Well, almost always right. Let's get going, Karis."

I started the engine, and off we drove.

About thirty minutes later, we pulled up outside a large, detached house.

"Someone's got a lot of money," Peggy pointed out. "I wonder if it's Johanna or Jerry. Maybe they have a lucrative murdering business."

We walked along the gravelled driveway to the imposing front door.

I said, "What are we going to say to Johanna if she answers the door?"

With a big smile on her face, Peggy replied, "I've already thought of that. Leave everything to me." She firmly knocked on the door.

It was answered by a dishevelled looking Johanna. Her eyes were red-rimmed, and there was barely any colour in her face.

She looked startled to see us, but quickly composed herself. "Oh. Hello. It's Karis, isn't it?"

"And me, Peggy Marshall. How are you doing after the unfortunate incident at the café?"

Johanna quickly blinked. "I'm still in shock. I didn't know the entertainer, of course, but it's still a very tragic situation. And for it to happen at little Primrose's party is beyond horrific."

"Indeed. Indeed." Peggy heaved a heartfelt sigh. "Can we talk to your husband, please?"

"My husband? What about?"

Peggy swiftly whipped her phone from her pocket. "I know he couldn't make it to the party, so I thought I'd show him some photos from that day. And I've got some videos too."

Johanna's look turned guarded. She rested her hand on the door as if getting ready to shut it in our faces. She said, "I've already shown him the photos I took."

"But I've got exclusive ones," Peggy persisted. "Ones taken behind the scenes which show the party being set up. I'm sure he'd like to see that. Also, I captured the moment Primrose came into the café. Her face lit up when she saw everything. You weren't there when that happened. I'm sure your hubby would like to see that."

I knew for certain Peggy didn't have such footage and photos of that time. In fact, I couldn't recall her taking any photos at all. I hoped Johanna didn't call her bluff and demand to see the photos and videos.

Luckily, she didn't. She said, "You can see him for a few moments. He's not very well. He suffers terribly from an old back injury. Seeing more photos of Primrose at her party might cheer him up. Follow me."

She opened the door wider to let us through. The inside of the house was just as magnificent as the outside. I had one of those awkward moments when I wondered if I should take my shoes off. Peggy looked as if she were thinking the same thing.

Johanna didn't say anything as she walked away, so we left our shoes on and followed her up the stairs.

When we got to the top, a phone rang out from a table at the bottom of the stairs.

Johanna said, "Excuse me a moment. That might be Klaudia. She could go into labour at any moment. But I don't know why she'd be ringing me on the house phone. Wait here, please." She headed back down the stairs.

My thoughts immediately went to Erin. I would phone her as soon as we'd finished here.

Peggy tugged on my sleeve, and hissed, "Quickly! Before she comes back."

"We don't know which room he's in."

"We'll soon find out." Still holding my sleeve, she rushed us along the landing.

Like contestants in a TV show, we opened one door after another expecting to see a man behind each one.

As we opened another unsuccessful door, Peggy muttered, "How many bedrooms does this house have?"

We persisted, and found Jerry behind the fifth door.

He was sitting up in bed reading a book. I was quite taken aback when he politely smiled, and said, "Hello. To what do I owe the pleasure?"

Peggy's reply was quick. "So sorry to disturb you. I'm Peggy Marshall, and this is Karis Booth. We work at Erin's Café. Where your granddaughter had her party." She was walking towards the bed at this stage, but stopped a moment to lower her head, and sadly add, "That tragic party." She lifted her head and continued moving towards the bed, and I thought for a moment that she was going to perch herself on the end of it.

Jerry put his book down. "Ah, yes. Poor Primrose. I hope she'll never find out what happened at her party."

I tilted my head towards the door. I could hear Johanna on the phone downstairs. She was telling someone very firmly that she didn't need double glazing, thank you very much. I reckoned it wouldn't be much longer before she was back upstairs.

I hurried over to Jerry and Peggy. Before Peggy could say another word, I blurted out, "We know about your past."

Jerry blanched. "My past? What do you mean?"

"Your clown past," I said. "Your clown name was Dazzle. Your career was soaring, and you were about to leave for America. But then you had an accident which put an end to your career. But it wasn't an accident. Your ankle was grabbed by Alvin Peel from behind some stage steps. He had an alibi, but he got someone to cover for him. You could never prove it was him. And the same Alvin Peel turned up to Primrose's party under your clown name." I stopped to catch my breath.

Peggy took up the onslaught of information. "Alvin was the clown who was killed at the café. Whoever did it made it look like a break-in gone wrong. But we know he was murdered. And we think—"

"Enough!" a voice called from the doorway. It was Johanna. Her face was flushed with anger. She repeated, "Enough! How dare you talk to my husband like that! I want you out of here right now!"

I looked at Jerry to see if he was going to say anything, but he turned away and stared at the wardrobe.

Johanna marched over to us looking like she was going to explode with anger. "Leave this room right now."

Peggy and I walked away from the bed and towards the door. My mind was awhirl with thoughts. Had Jerry murdered Alvin? Was he even the man previously known as Dazzle?

Before we left the room, I cast a look back at Jerry. He was still staring at the wardrobe. For a moment, I thought I saw tears in his eyes. He caught me looking, and turned his head away.

Johanna firmly closed the bedroom door behind us, and then pointed to the stairs ahead.

Once we were downstairs, I expected her to fling us out of the front door. But she didn't.

"Come this way," she ordered. She took us into an expensively decorated living room. Closing the door behind us, she lifted her chin and said, "I killed Alvin Peel."

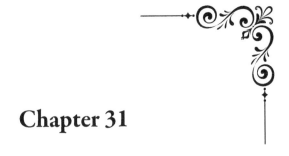

Chapter 31

"I knew it!" Peggy declared as she looked at Johanna.

"Pardon?" Johanna said.

Peggy planted her hands on her hips. "I knew there was something devious about you, as if you were keeping a big secret."

Johanna looked shocked. "Devious?"

"Yes. Through and through," Peggy added. "So, tell us why you did it."

A hardness came into Johanna's eyes. "If you're such an expert on me, why don't you tell me why I did it?" She moved over to the sofa, and sat down crossing one slim leg over the other.

Peggy suddenly seemed less sure, and her hands left her hips. "Well, it's obvious. After what Alvin said to Dean about him not being the father of Klaudia's children, well, it's no wonder you were mad enough to kill him."

"Really? Is that what you think?" Considering Johanna had just admitted to killing someone, she was remarkably calm.

Peggy said, "Yes, that's what I think. And I don't blame you for being annoyed with Alvin. He had a nasty streak running through him."

"I didn't kill him because of that," Johanna stated calmly. "Do take a seat, the both of you. Would you like some refreshments?"

Peggy and I shared an incredulous look, and shook our heads at the same time. It seemed neither of us wanted to take tea with a killer.

We sat in armchairs in front of the sofa, and waited for Johanna to continue.

Johanna said, "I killed Alvin Peel because of what he did to Jerry. How much do you know about my husband's past? I didn't quite catch all the nasty words you were throwing at him upstairs."

I said, "About him being a clown called Dazzle? And that he worked with Alvin back in the day? Yes, we know about that."

Peggy added, "And we know your husband suffered an accident at the hands of Alvin, but it could never be proved. And that accident put paid to his career."

Johanna slowly nodded. "You know a lot. But not everything. When I met Jerry, I didn't know anything about his clown career. And he's never spoken to anyone about it. He was working in pensions and investments when we met. He retired recently. Having a desk job suited him because of the back pain he's been plagued with since that accident." She fell silent as if not willing to give us any more information.

"How did you find out about his clown career?" I prompted.

She gave us a slow smile. "Why do husbands think they can keep anything from their wives? Especially when they've been married for as long as Jerry and I have. There were so many clues over the years. How his face lit up whenever he saw a clown, even on the television. And how much he knew about the history of clowns. He would often regale me for hours about that. His face was aglow when he spoke about them and all the unwritten rules they have. I could see how passionate he was about them. But it was the dressing up which confirmed it."

"Dressing up?" Peggy repeated. "Women's clothes? Yours?"

"Not women's clothes. Clown clothes. Or outfits, I suppose that's the right word to use. Because of his bad back, we sleep in separate rooms. Once, I'd heard him moving about in the night. I assumed he was in pain, so I headed to his bedroom to see if I could help in any way. But when I looked through a gap in the door, I saw him dressed up in a sparkly clown outfit. He even had a bit of face paint on." Her voice caught in her throat. "He had his back to me, and he was silently performing as if to an invisible audience. He even took bows."

That sad image made my eyes sting a little. Until I remembered I was talking to a murderer.

Johanna continued, "I was curious, so I hired a private detective who found out about Jerry's past. I couldn't stop crying when I was given all the facts. What a terrible thing to happen to the man I love so dearly."

I asked, "Did you tell him you'd found out about his past?"

She shook her head. "I didn't. I was tempted, but I reasoned that if he wanted me to know, then he'd tell me. As well as finding out about Jerry's past, I also discovered what Alvin Peel had done to him. The private detective found out Alvin's alibi for the time of the accident wasn't real. He'd got a former girlfriend to lie for him. Again, I wanted to tell Jerry, but I was worried what that information would do to him."

"When did you decide to kill Alvin?" Peggy carefully asked.

"When I saw him at that party. The detective had given me photos of Alvin, and what his clown name was." Her face twisted in anger. "I couldn't believe it when Alvin took on Jerry's clown name, and even his clown outfit and make-up. What an evil specimen he was. When I saw him at the party, despite the face paint, I knew immediately who he was. I confronted him in the kitchen, but all he did was laugh. And then he made vulgar comments about how Jerry must be a useless husband now, just before he made a pass at me." She wiped her cheek as if cleaning away the memory of Alvin touching her.

Just as carefully as Peggy, I asked, "Did you mean to kill him?"

"No, it was an accident. After his second performance, I followed him into the kitchen to tell him he was a disgrace, and that I was going to tell everyone he was a fraud. He lunged at me, and I panicked. I pushed him away, and he fell on that cake. I didn't know he'd fallen on the unicorn's horn. As soon as he fell, I ran out of the kitchen. I didn't know he was dead until later."

"Why didn't you tell Seb about this?" I asked.

She shrugged. "Because I thought Alvin deserved to die. And I didn't want to upset Jerry by telling him it was me who killed him." She sighed heavily. "But I'm ready to tell the police now."

I looked at Peggy. The expression on her face confirmed she was thinking the same thing as me.

I gave Johanna a direct look, and said, "You didn't kill Alvin Peel."

"I did. It was me! And that's what I'm going to tell the police."

I shook my head. "They won't believe you. Not when I tell them who the real killer is."

Chapter 32

Johanna protested some more, but we didn't listen. And when we walked towards the door, she attempted to block our exit. Foolishly, she put her hand on Peggy's shoulder to stop her from leaving. But she was no match for Peggy's sharp elbows which had got her through many a crowd, particularly those who fill the shops at Christmas.

Johanna was still shouting at us as we headed for the stairs.

We stopped when we saw Jerry coming down the stairs. He said, "Johanna love, what's all the shouting about?"

"Nothing. Go back to bed."

"I can't. I've got something to say to these ladies." He reached the ground, and looked at us. "You were right about everything you said upstairs. About me being a clown, and Alvin Peel causing my accident." His attention went to Johanna. "I suspect you know about my past. Am I right?"

Tears sprang to Johanna's eyes. "I do know. I've known for a while."

Jerry took his wife in his arms and kissed her. He released her, and said softly, "I should have told you years ago. I'm so sorry. But I didn't want to bring my past up, not when we were starting our life together. Can you ever forgive me?"

"There's nothing to forgive," Johanna replied. "I should have told you I knew. We could have shared that part of your life."

Jerry let out a small laugh. "We've been so stupid, haven't we. Keeping this secret to ourselves when it wasn't really a secret at all." He kissed her again, and turned to us. "It was me who killed Alvin Peel."

"No!" Johanna declared. "Don't say another word. I've already confessed to his murder."

Jerry frowned. "You have? Why?"

Her eyes filled with tears. "You've been through enough. That despicable man deserved to die after what he did to you. He took your passion away." Tears trickled down her cheeks.

"My passion?" Jerry asked.

"Yes. Your passion for performing as a clown. I know how successful you were, and about the American offer."

Jerry tenderly wiped her tears away, and said, "My sweet love, my passion is for you and our beautiful family. I'm thankful my career as a clown was cut short. If it hadn't been, I wouldn't have met you. And that would have been a tragedy."

She shook her head. "I can't let you confess to his murder. I just can't. I don't want to lose you."

"You'll never lose me. I'll always be around, even if I'm behind bars." He looked into her eyes. "How long have you known it was me who killed him?"

"I knew as soon as the police told me he was dead." Her smile at Jerry was full of sadness. "I knew you were in the café somewhere. Do you remember those apps you downloaded onto our phones? The ones where we can locate each other? When you're having bad days, I often check it to make sure you're still at home."

"Spying on me?" he said with a smile.

Johanna nodded. "You've only yourself to blame. How many times have I told you to stay in bed and rest, and then I come home to find you've left the house to do favours for other people? I was so annoyed with Alvin at the party, and my thoughts went to you. So, I checked the app and saw you were in the street at the rear of the café. It didn't take me long to work out what had happened. Was it an accident? Did he say horrible things to you?"

Jerry sighed. "He did. I only meant to talk to him, but things got out of hand. I've been watching his career for years even though it consumed me with anger. He has lots of videos online, and the sight of his smug face made my blood boil. When I found out he'd taken my name and identity, I–" He stopped talking while he composed himself. "I thought that was bad enough, but when he had the nerve to perform at Primrose's party, I couldn't take it any longer. I had to speak to him."

"Did he know about the family connection? With Primrose and you?" I asked.

Jerry gave me a long look. "He did. He gloated about it just before we got into a fight. I didn't go there planning to fight with him. I was going to demand he give up my name voluntarily. And if he wouldn't, I was going to publicly shame him. But my temper got the better of me. He goaded me, and then insulted my family. It was too much. I couldn't control my actions. We got into a fight, and he fell onto that unicorn cake. When he didn't move, I thought he was messing about. But he was dead. I panicked, and made his death look like a burglary."

Something wasn't adding up.

I said, "What about the CCTV cameras?"

"What cameras?" Jerry asked too innocently.

"The ones outside the café. The ones you sprayed with paint."

"I don't know what you're talking about." His tone remained innocent.

"The CCTV cameras," I persisted. "You sabotaged them so you wouldn't be seen. You were dressed in your clown outfit. The cameras were damaged an hour before the party took place. You planned to kill Alvin. It wasn't an accident."

"Jerry?" Johanna asked. "Did you plan to kill him before you got to the café?"

For a moment, it looked like Jerry was going to deny it. But then he said, "I did. I had to get rid of him for good. I knew he'd never agree to giving my identity up. I'd always known he was behind my accident. He had to pay for what he'd done. All those hours spent in bed because of my bad back fuelled me with plans of revenge. I wasn't sure I was going to kill him, but a few seconds in his presence, and I knew I had to. He was a vile man."

Johanna nodded. "He was. Please, Jerry, let me take the blame. You've been so good to me over the years, and it's time I did something for you."

"No. I won't allow it. You need to stay here with our family. You have to be strong. And you have to do something about Klaudia and Dean, and their complicated love lives. Johanna, phone the police for me. Please."

She burst into tears, reached for her husband and hugged him tightly.

I was about to say something, but a fierce pain gripped my stomach, knocking the breath out of me.

Peggy was instantly alert. She grabbed my arm. "Karis! What's wrong?"

Another pain shot through me. It was a familiar one even though I hadn't experienced it for over two decades.

Through gritted teeth, I said, "I have to go. It's Erin. Something's happening to her."

Chapter 33

Peggy assured me she would stay with Jerry and Johanna until the police arrived. Then she phoned Seb who said he'd be there in five minutes. I hated to leave Peggy, but the pain in my stomach kept returning, and getting stronger. I wasn't even sure I'd be able to drive, but I had to get to my sister immediately.

I didn't get very far with my journey because once I got into my car, the pain became too strong, causing me to double over. There was no doubt I was experiencing Erin's labour pains. Did it mean she was in labour? Or about to go into labour?

The pain faded, so I decided to phone for a taxi as I couldn't drive in my condition. I almost jumped out of my skin when there was a tap on the driver's window.

It was Seb. I lowered the window, and said, "I'm going into labour — Erin's labour." I winced as another contraction got ahold of me.

Seb nodded, and said something to a man behind him. Then he opened the driver's door, and gently led me around to the passenger side. I gritted my teeth as the contraction reached its peak, and then fell away. I felt like screaming, and thought I probably would when the next contraction hit me.

Seb placed me in the passenger seat and put the seat belt over me. Then he quickly got into the driver's seat and sped away.

I braced myself for another contraction, but nothing came. Except for a wave of worry about Erin. Had something happened to her? Labour pains shouldn't be over so quickly.

I said to Seb, "Can you drive faster?"

He nodded, and the car shot forward.

By the time we pulled up outside Erin's house, I was releasing my seat belt and had my hand on the door. As soon as we came to a stop, I was out of the car and running towards the house. My heart almost stopped when I saw the back door was wide open. I raced inside.

"Erin!" I yelled. "Erin! Where are you?"

"We're up here!" Robbie cried out. "In the bedroom."

I ran up the stairs. Seb followed me.

I came to a stop outside the open bedroom door, suddenly afraid of what I might find inside.

Seb placed his arm around my shoulders, and said, "Come on. You can't just stand there."

"I can." I stared at the door.

He gently led me inside.

I almost stopped breathing when I saw the scene in front of me.

Erin was sitting up in bed, her face flushed. Robbie was at her side, his face was aglow. Each of them was holding a baby wrapped in a blanket.

Robbie smiled as he looked our way. His voice was full of awe as he said, "They came. So quickly. So very quickly. Look. I've got a son."

"And a daughter," Erin said softly. They looked at each other with so much love that my heart almost melted.

Seb slipped his hand into mine, and we walked towards the new family.

I said, "What happened? I started feeling your contractions twenty minutes ago. They were bad."

"You're telling me," Erin said. "They started out of nowhere. Just all of a sudden. I was scared stiff. I didn't know what to do. I managed to phone Robbie, and he was here within minutes."

Robbie took up the tale. "When I came in here, the babies were already on the way. And I—" He fell silent, and gazed at Erin in wonder.

Erin said, "He was wonderful. Calm. Controlled. He delivered our babies."

"You did all the work," Robbie said.

"I didn't do that much. It was a very short labour. I think our little ones were eager to meet us."

They gazed at each other again, before looking at their son and daughter who were sleeping peacefully.

Ever the worrier, I said, "Have you phoned for an ambulance? Erin, you need to be checked over, and the babies should be examined." I glanced at Robbie. "I think your husband needs to be examined too. He looks in shock."

"I am in shock," Robbie said. "But it's a lovely shock."

Seb and I moved closer to the bed. He squeezed my hand gently as we looked at the beautiful babies.

Then I burst into tears. Big, fat happy tears. Seb put his arm around me.

Peggy rushed into the room. "What have I missed now?"

Through my tears, I said, "The start of a new adventure."

About the author

I live in a county called Yorkshire, England with my family. This area is known for its paranormal activity and haunted dwellings. I love all things supernatural and think there is more to this life than can be seen with our eyes.

I HOPE YOU ENJOYED this story. If you did, I'd love it if you could post a small review. Reviews really help authors to sell more books. Thank you!

THIS STORY HAS BEEN checked for errors by myself and my team. If you spot anything we've missed, you can let us know by emailing us at: april@aprilfernsby.com

YOU CAN VISIT MY WEBSITE at: www.aprilfernsby.com[1]

FOLLOW ME ON Bookbub[2]
   Warm wishes
   April Fernsby

---

1. http://www.aprilfernsby.com

2. https://www.bookbub.com/authors/april-fernsby

A Tragic Party
A Psychic Café Mystery
(Book 6)
By
April Fernsby
www.aprilfernsby.com

Don't miss out!

Visit the website below and you can sign up to receive emails whenever April Fernsby publishes a new book. There's no charge and no obligation.

https://books2read.com/r/B-A-LQJE-JQKCB

BOOKS 2 READ

Connecting independent readers to independent writers.

Also by April Fernsby

Standalone
Murder Of A Werewolf
The Leprechaun's Last Trick
A Fatal Wedding
Psychic Cafe Mysteries Box Set 1
Brimstone Witch Mysteries - Box Set 1
Brimstone Witch Mysteries - Box Set 2
Brimstone Witch Mysteries - Box Set 3
Brimstone Witch Mysteries - Box Set 4
Brimstone Witch Mysteries - Books 1 to 13

Lightning Source UK Ltd.
Milton Keynes UK
UKHW010630180722
406010UK00001B/194

9 781393 961345